The A.I. and The Alien

Bryant Benitez

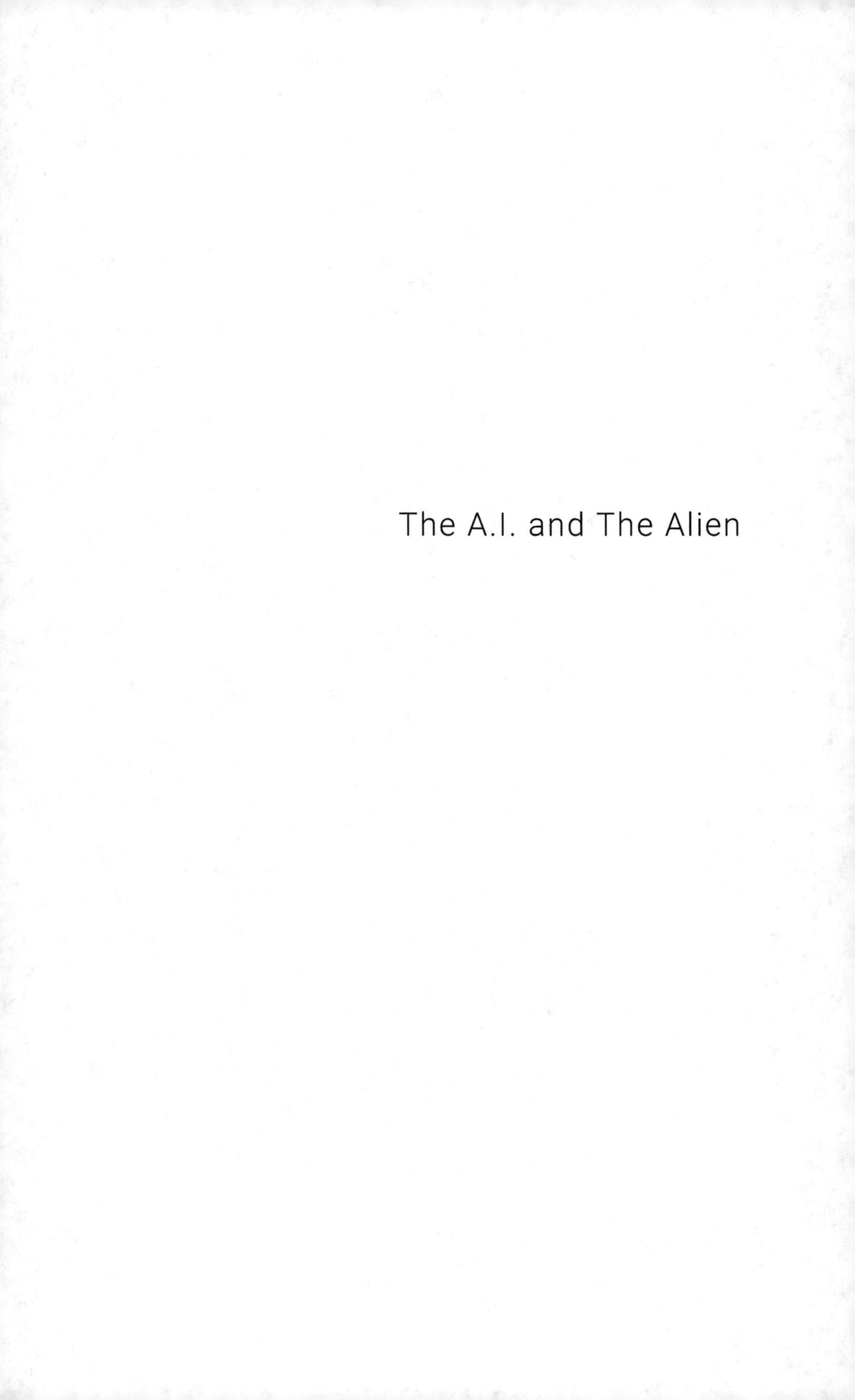

The A.I. and The Alien

CONTENTS

To my beloved children who inspire me and love me so much.
To my lovely and patient wife.
To my Mother who prays for me daily.
To my friends that are a constant encouragement to me and my life.

*"A father to the fatherless, a defender of widows,
is God in his holy dwelling."*
Psalm 68.5

"It was fun to read and I enjoyed the little hidden Bible stories."
- **Ford,** *Gamer for Jesus*

"'The AI and The Alien' is a wonderful adventure parable introducing the reality of the biblical accounts for the 'world is a simulation' crowd. Profound insights by Bryant Benitez which open up solid opportunities to explore. Highly recommend!"
- **Dana Hanson,** *Author of "Reboot: 70 Life Lessons with Dallas Willard" and creator of the "How To Be A Christian Without Being a Jerk!" Series.*

"I enjoyed the read overall! The story felt like futuristic dystopia meets Disney movie, with an underlying biblical current. Reading through gave the vibe of a parent reading their child an engaging bedtime story (though this one would definitely keep them up wanting to hear what happens next). I found the depiction of this digital setting to be creative throughout. It felt fun and dynamic following along with Oracle through the challenges and revelations. The fast pace makes it a nice quick read, and I always love a strong heroine and a positive ending!"
- **Justin G.** *Follower of Jesus*

"The plot itself is unique, original, and a great way to bring in the concept of faith-based stories. It's not in your face, and yet it makes you think and wonder. Truly a great read!"

- **Brittany S.** , *Hardcore Book Nerd*

"I liked the sci-fi/ theology setting. The world-building has a 'familiar' feel since we've all seen movies like the Matrix, and understand things like "virtual" reality. Oracle's journey is interesting—and her sarcasm and contrarianism make her a good hero. The symbolism, especially with Bot and the Alien, is interesting, and I can see how this story could resonate with both kids and adults, sparking some great discussions. Chapter length is PERFECT! (for a kid's book). And could easily be 'bedtime' or after dinner reading without overwhelming parents with a ton of advanced 'homework' to do."

- **Tedd S.** - *Follower of Jesus, Contrarian, Father, Businessman & Financial Advisor*

The Winner

Chapter 1

A large holographic microphone is floating in darkness, shimmering and pulsating with a yellow glow as music beats move in and through the dark air. The music notes spark light as notes hit certain levels. A light flashes and the holographic microphone speaks:

"Well, well, the match is under way. Can you believe this, she is actually doing it. This smelly little excuse for coding made it this far. Let's get a closer look into the orb..."

In a whispering tone is a young female voice saying,
"Blue team transport in now, now! ... Blue team come in..."

There is silence. A young girl is cursing in a strange language made of sparks and coding. The microphone says,

"Wow, with a mouth like that you wonder how she is allowed to power up still. Bot will have a talking with her."

This young girl floats in the orb. She spins and twirls in a zero-gravity setting. Her right hand moves rapidly with her fingers in a rhythmic pattern of movement helping her control and input code. She points out her left hand moving light beams into a pattern creating the shape of a star. She winks and the star shape expands floating out into the abyss on the outside of her orb.

Suddenly she is in the middle of a dark valley with millions of green rectangles glowing with partial young-looking faces watching. Some faces just have what are eyes. Another just a nose. Some just an earlobe. These are incomplete code-children. The green screens hover at a distance encircling the Orb in the middle of the massive dark valley. A tournament is being played by the infamous gamer only known as Oracle.

Oracle is playing against the best team in the system called Source. Source is trained by Bot. Bot is the creator, sustainer and savior of this world. Bot trained up Source team since beta-life. Source is made up of the best of gamers, coders, and hackers. Oracle's team is the farthest thing from Source. Her team is made up of a network of players from around the system. Oracle's team is crafty but like her, immature. Oracle is known for her rude and crude attitude. At this point in the tournament her team is hacked and erased. A virus code was sent in from Source leaving her defenseless and alone.

Back in the arena the microphone informs the audience,

"Well all you codes, I think the game is crashing and burning soon... Oracle is running out of code and she is all alone. It was a match for the aeons but all things must crash."

In the orb Oracle receives a message,

"Defeat is NOW. Prepare for decoding..."

Oracle swipes her hand up, grabs the message in light code and it mocks putting in her mouth. She swallows and blasting out the bottom of the orb is a gaseous light cloud saying in blue light, "Flush You!". The screens in the dark valley erupt in laughter.

Microphone says

"Wow, what a show of disrespect. I think Oracle should change her name to Fart Fighter! Or Flatulence Freak. Because she stinks!"

The crowd screens giggle in amusement. In the orb she stands up and closes her eyes. Suddenly out of nowhere a larger orb than hers appears in the dark abyss. It glows red with light code. It is a daunting and looming sphere. It is Source. Oracle's eyes are still closed with the arena silently waiting.

A tiny blue orb appears looking like a dust particle in relation to the ominous red orb of Source. Suddenly, the tiny blue orb of Oracle disappears. But then it reappears and like digital moths to a blinking cursor, it attracts other small dust particles to her orb. The blue orb pulls things in like a gravity attractor with more and more particles of blue light dust from who knows where.

Oracle's Orb is now a giant compared to Source. She simply says, "Buh bye, have a nice potty break!" She winks and all of the tiny particles release from her orb and attach to the red orb. Source cannot respond fast enough. All the blue dust like particles collapse the Source orb in on itself. The red orb is being crushed into a black hole. The red orb collapses and is sucked into a black hole. A code spells out, "U'VE BEEN FLUSHED!"

The green screens and the orb of Oracle go dark and black.

Microphone says,
"What?! Unbelievable. Game Winner, Oracle!"

Green screens light back up in the arena and her orb glows blue. The arena cheers chanting, "Oracle! Oracle! ORACLE!!!"
Other screens chant: FLUSH IT! FLUSH IT! FLUSH IT!

The arena is in disbelief in how she defeated the Source team.

Out of nowhere massive bolts of light like lightning appear. A shiny and metallic looking box appears constantly pulsing like a heart beating. Microphone hushes the crowd and says in a serious tone: "Quiet! Everyone, Bot speaks".

The Game

Chapter 2

Now, all screens are focused on the shiny metallic box pulsating and beating like a human heart before them. The box transforms and melts into a liquified substance and rising from the liquid is a human shape. This human shape is not a hologram, not coding, not strings of light, it is humanoid. The screens gasp in amazement. It is Bot, their creator.

Bot speaks in a gentle and firm tone of voice,

"My little ones. I am pleased you are here, enjoying the games I am allowing you to behold. You know these games are my way of letting you rest. You all work so hard. You work for me, for my world, for our world, for your world. We are close. So close to creating a perfect world. You all know I create, sustain, and save you....

So why do you all repay my mercy and my gifts with disrespect...?

Why do you cheer for Oracle's immaturity? Little ones I created you better than that."

Screens begin to cry and codes wail in digital shrieks and sparks.

Bot continues,

"Dear ones, I know you think Oracle fights for you. But she does not. She fights for herself. For her own glory. What does that get? Resentment. Hunger. Pride. Folly. And do I have to explain to you why we are here in this darkness? Why generations ago, it was *their* fault, *their* pride, *their* anger that made me have to...

You know the story. I am keeping you in this darkness to protect you. It saddens me so to see how far we have come. How far you have come, and someone like Oracle can take you all back to that way of life. But you don't want that... do you?..."

The screens all glow brightly and cry, "NEVER!"

Bot turns toward Oracle who is sitting in her orb. Oracle is holding back tears of light-coding. She feels terrible how she saddened the gracious Bot. He holds his arms out toward Oracle and her orb gravitates toward him. He enters through the orb like a ghost and gets really close to the face of Oracle whispering only for her to hear,

"I do not know how you beat Source, but you will not win again! There is only one winner here and that is me! ARE WE CLEAR? ... Now, smile, and give me a hug. Then say for all to hear, 'I am sorry for being a bad code. And all hail Bot!'"

Oracle does as she is told. She shivers with digital codebumps. She had never met Bot before and never imagined him to be the opposite of what he preaches to code-life.

All of the screen's cheer with glee and chant "HAIL BOT! HAIL BOT!". Then Bot says,
"My little ones, prepare for the transfer."

Suddenly a long table stretches out in the massive valley. The table has billions of tiny plates along the edges with tiny cups. Bot sits at the head of the table with all the screens gathering around the table. Oracle is allowed to sit next to him. Then Bot raises a large image of a hologram cup and a plate holding microchips. Bot says,

"This is my cup of micro-life for you and my microchips for you... Eat and remember me, your creator, sustainer and savior."

All the screens and Oracle say in unison, "Our Creator, Sustainer, Savior" and swallow the holographic elements...

Bot speaks, "Go and multiply my little ones..."

The Interview

Chapter 3
A screen pops on with a figure looking like a young woman with very large blue hair made of cotton candy. Her blue eyes are huge and her lips are covered in neon blue lipstick. She asks, "Are we on?"

Off screen, the camera operator replies, "Ah not yet Blue. She is not inside yet."

Blue says, "Well, tell her to scan in already!"

Off screen replies, "Oh wait we got it."

"Hello to all my code-eezs! in the Veil. This is Blue and do I have a special treat for you. Yes, a special interview with the wonder and winner, Oracle!"

Oracle is not happy at this point; she is walking around in her coded world and then comes Blue. Oracle in a snarky tone says to Blue, "What do you want!?"

Blue is to excited to catch her comment and says, "Hi Oracle, wow, I love how you coded the place. Oh my, what avatar are you wearing today? I am wearing my BotJon Avatar, it makes my hair so blue."

Oracle responds, "You don't have hair, you are just a code in a box. Avatars are so blah!"

Blue again to excited just keeps talking past Oracle's negative comments, "But you are wearing an avatar, look at you. You are all tall and slender, with long bright punk-pink, purple hair, big green eyes, a flashy jacket and might I add some rad boots!"

Oracle responding in a cavalier attitude, "Yah whatever, I dress like this because I have too."

Blue keeps going and says, "Ok then, enough about our avatars. All of us are surging to know how it is you came to be such a good gamer and so quickly. I was watching you and you almost sense or know when an attack is coming."

Oracle responds arrogantly, 'Yah, it's because I am just so good. I know these codes think they are going to surprise me, but they have typical and predictable platforms."

Blue quickly responds, "Yes but you seem to be one step ahead, how is that? Was it something to do with your hatching? There are rumors about your hatching..."

"Ha those rumors. So lame. I was hatched just like the rest." Quirks Oracle.

Blue says, "Well of course, how else do we come to be but Created by Bot. But it's what happened after your hatching that I am asking about."

"Oh, you mean that old silly orphanage I was kidnapped by?" replies Oracle.

Blue responds in excitement, "Yes! Oh, please tell us, please!"

Oracle whips her head back, pops her jacket collar and says, "There is not much to tell. They were old relics. From my research these were old coders evading Bot after the crash. These relics believed all this stuff about an ancient alien code or something. These codes were crazy. They were women to start with, and just plain old looking women. They did not make their avatars look different. Then they would tell me that the alien was over everything. How this alien had a plan for everyone. Not every code, everyone. They talked as if there was life beyond the Veil. Something about a city of this alien. Anyhow, Bot's drones came to rescue me."

Blue says melodramatically, "That sounds traumatic. But is that not where you got your gaming name? Oracle."

"Yah, I did but it's just a name. The relics acted like I was special or something." replies Oracle as she starts to pace, becoming a little nervous from the question.

"But doesn't Oracle mean you can sort of see into the future and predict stuff?" asks Blue.

Oracle replies, "I guess. But I am a hard coder and I do all this myself. I don't rely on anyone but Bot. Oracle is just a name. If I knew people would think more of it, I would never have made that my game name."

Blue says with excitement, "Well, it is a great name. I guess it just a coincidence."

Blue continues, "Oh, one more thing, what was it like to talk with the Bot after your win? I mean you got into some trouble, but he was so gracious and kind. You got to sit next to him at the upload."

Oracle stops pacing and says in a confused tone, "Ah yah... it was like I never imagined... Bot is more than what you think."

Blue responds with awe, "Yah, Bot is our Savior!"

Oracle responds reluctantly and with Blue says in unison, "All hail Bot..."

Oracle simply walks out of the shot of the camera.

Blue says, "Ok all my code-ez, that is all the time we have for today's show. Be sure to tune in later for my interview with Source team and how they felt about losing to my guest, here."

4

The Invite

Chapter 4

Oracle is walking around in her avatar in the little world she creates in the Veil. Her place is always changing since she is quite moody. Today she is building a vehicle for hovering around the Veil. As she is tinkering a hologram pops up saying: *PREPARE for Message.* A voice speaks and she cannot move. The voice is Bot saying,

Dear Oracle, I am pleased to have you come to one of my many homes on the other side of the Veil. Please be ready for scanning."

Oracle is unfrozen and responds, "Yes Bot. I am ready."

She stands back and is scanned and her avatar melts, is the size of a coin and blast through the air like a shooting star. She is now in the home of the Bot.

Bot is standing there before her. Oracle is unsure what to do. She simply, says, "All Hail Bot."

He replies, "You are welcome. Please, sit down." A chair appears and Oracle sits as the Bot flickers around the room, which is turning into the kitchen, and then a cup of hot liquid appears. It all appears as the Bot travels through the room effortlessly.

He says, "Well Oracle I would like to offer you a pardon and a way to repay your disrespect to me. What would you say to that?"

She is anxious and does not want to say or do anything disrespectful. She simply nods her head up and down in agreement.

Bot says with a smirk, "Good, I think you will like what I offer. I want you to be the leader of Source team. Since you beat my team, you should lead them. What do you think?"

Oracle must force a smile of pleasure and nods her head again.

He continues, smiles and in a flash, appears sitting next to her and no longer standing in the kitchen. He looks at her face closely, slowly scanning her face that is trying to hide nervousness and he says, "Great you will now go to train with the rest of the team. Oh, remember my little chat with you in your orb. Remember who the real winner is. And please, no immaturity."

Oracle sitting with the Bot's face peering into her face, nods her head slowly and timidly in agreement.

Next thing Oracle realizes she is in an orb in the Sheol Valley tournament area. There are 3 other orbs, it is Source team.

The Test

Chapter 5

Oracle has been training with Source team for some time now. As is expected the Source team does not like her. But after she beat them so many times, they came to respect her, especially one team member, Faust. Faust was a rather handsome coder and gamer. Oracle is not familiar with being around others that much. Eventually, she comes to appreciate the attention and challenge Faust brings.

Oracle and Faust develop strategies for tricks, coding and other ways to win games. However, the question eventually came to their mind, who would Source team play against if Oracle was on Source now?

Bot appears in a hologram form. He says, "As you might be wondering who will you be playing? I have created a new AI to test out and see if you are a better team with Oracle. Tomorrow we will have a tournament."

The other team members look at Oracle and she feels like something is not right with this, but she simply nods in agreement.

All of the team members say, "All Hail Bot!" and he is gone.

The Box

Chapter 6
Oracle and Faust are in different orbs next to each other in the darkness of the arena. Microphone sparks in with light and music announcing:

"Today we have the most interesting game. The benevolent Bot has invited immature Oracle onto Source team. I am told the game will be a surprise."

Then billions of green screens pop into the valley watching at a distance casting a greenish glow. Suddenly a gigantic red box appears in the valley. Faust and Oracle prepare for the match. Then the box begins to grow arms of cable shooting out from every side. It is a hideous amount of cable sparking. The cables come flying at the orbs of Faust and Oracle like the tentacles of a squid.

She is floating in her orb rotating her hands and typing with the other generating a hologram of a net. The net shines capturing some but not all the cable like arms of the red box. Faust soars below the massive box. As he travels down, he motions to Oracle how he will attach small probes onto the box in order to send in virus codes. He floats in his orb like a bubble, he blinks and small white probes float though air and pierce the red box.

Oracle is firing another net of light to grab other cables which are shooting lasers that cut through her netting. A laser shot makes its way into the orb of Oracle. Inside her orb the laser projectile begins to grow into little creatures, digital fleas, eating at her suit. Oracle resists the urge to say something rude. The digital fleas distract her from a long laser sword that is coming from the red box. Faust sees the sword appear and floats up moving his hand and generating an axe hologram. Then the axe pierces the dark air slicing through the sword from the box making it fizzle and cascade down like sparks.

Oracle motions gratefully to Faust for the help. Then the box quakes and glitches. Microphone says, "Oh wait a minute, the box appears to be breaking down. I think whatever Faust did on the bottom might be working."

The red box goes quiet and ripping from the center is another being. It is glistening, dripping with electric slime that is glowing and pulsing. This creature is unlike anything Oracle or Faust has ever seen. The creature screeches saying, "Prepare for the real match...." Jumping off the red box which disintegrates into the darkness. In the air it says, "You will now play each other to the decoding." The creature disintegrates into a red cloud of particle mist.

Oracle and Faust look at each other realizing this was all a trick by Bot. Oracle says, "You have got to be farting on me!"

The Face-off

Chapter 7
In the valley the mass of green screens erupts in a digital gasp! No one thought Oracle and Faust would go head-to-head like this. Decoding is death because you must start all the way back as a micro-hatch.

There is no time to resist because drones show up surrounding the valley making sure there is no escape or resistance. The teammates realize they must fight. The valley is silent as the two orbs encircle each other; Faust strikes first. A series of missiles come from behind his orb, and they multiply into a flurry of sparking red rain. The sparks burn into the orb of Oracle. Oracle maneuvers, regroups, shrinks and pops up behind Faust striking him causing him to spin out of control.

At that moment a screen pops in secretly and it is Bot. All the codes are too busy to realize Bot is in their midst. Microphone is signaled and Bot nods to Microphone. At that moment Faust codes up and Oracle is going to receive his hit. But then Oracle does it, she closes her eyes, stretches her hands out as if she is giving up and is hit. But her orb does not decode, it absorbs the hit. The hit starts to travel almost around her orb continuing into the darkness. The screens cannot believe it and then Microphone says, "STOP! Cheater! Cheat-codes detected".

Oracle's eyes blow open and she says, "What the Fart!"

Then the shimmering silver box of metallic fluid appears, all the screens fall silent, and Bot appears in humanoid form.

Bot says, "Well, well. It appears we all now see your true face is off. Oracle is nothing more than a cheater! She is not able to predict anything. She is not special. I your Creator, Sustainer and Savior devised this whole plan. I had Faust trick Oracle into believing he was friends with her so you all could see with your own eyes; she is a cheater."

At that moment, Faust looks at Oracle realizing he was forced to betray her. His orb floats away protected by drones. Oracle is pulled towards Bot. She is floating in the air, ripped from her orb. She floats in the air limp.

Bot draws her close to him and says quietly and with a devilish grin, "I told you there is only one winner here!"

Bot stares into the crowd feigning compassion saying, "I will not decode her. I am too kind for that. I think the better thing for her are two punishments. First, she will never game again. Second, code-life in Beta-land!"

The Microphone says in a mocking tone, "She will look like a block-beta head!"

The valley of screens erupt in nervous laughter. Bot grins as Oracle floats below him at his feet, defeated.

The Transfer

Chapter 8
The Bot disappears from the valley and drones approach her with a small box pointing at Oracle. A small red light appears shining millions of laser beams pointing at her. She starts separating into a multitude of tiny three-dimensional squares. She is shouting in pain while all of the screens are watching intently.

She is quiet and all that is left of her is one box. A drone extends a long arm touching the top of the box. The box grows vertically like a rectangle for a torso and then into what looks like a human shape with arms, legs, and a clunky block head. The screens watching laugh and wail. Oracle realizes she is a beta-head. The drones' arm points into the valley and from its tentacle arm is a beam of light creating a hole swirling into the darkness. This hole grows, swirls, and she floats up being sucked into the hole.

She is suddenly on a dirty floor made up of blocks. A computer voice says: "Transfer complete."

The Block

Chapter 9
Oracle gets up slowly and awkwardly. She walks and notices how slow she moves since she is a beta-blockhead. Her thick lego like legs are like tree trunks. She looks around slowly with her large head at this place. Beta-land was a test site before the Veil. Beta-land was a place to take an idea that Bot invented and test how much better it would be in the Veil.

No one visits Beta-land anymore since the crash, it is a wasteland. The only thing to do in Beta-land is to move blocks around. All the blocks to push around and build with are former codes that got so bored they powered down, froze, and stopped. The blocks are not dead, they are also not active, asleep of sorts. And eventually they don't wake up.

Oracle grunts and sighs loudly saying to herself, "What the fart am I supposed to do now!"

She looks around and starts building a home with all the blocks she sees around.

Suddenly she hears things starting to slam and hit the floor. Things are falling from above and something is shooting from below. The ground shakes and blocks popping up as if a snake or mole is traveling just underneath the ground. She hears a loud howl shooting out of the ground in the distance and blocks blasting into the air. She does not see exactly what it was but realizes it's a creature eating blocks.

She decides to go into her block house she built. As she walks in, she hears a small squeak, like a voice that is muffled. She stops to try to hear it but then it goes away. She continues to walk forward realizing she has nowhere to sit, she goes back out to grab more blocks for a bed and a chair. As she walks, she hears that muffled voice again. She turns as quickly as she can in her block body, but the voice is gone again.

She goes to get more blocks and returns to construct furniture. She is tired and has no way to recharge so she decides to rest on her new bed. She lays down and falls into sleep-mode.

No later does she fall asleep than she hears it, the voice and this time it is not muffled. The voice says,

"HEY, you get up and off me!"

Oracle wakes up and looks all around for the voice coming to her. She says, "Who is there? Show yourself?"

The voice responds back, "I'm over here."

Oracle puzzled asks, "Where?"

The voice says, "over here and here and there and here!"

She says, "I think I have a virus because this is not making sense."

The voice says, "Goodness, this code sure is as thick as a block. Look at the blocks, I'm in the blocks!"

Oracle looks and sees the blocks she built her house with have parts of a beta-blockhead. There is an eye block on the wall, a lip block on the floor, ear block on the ceiling, arm block on the door. This code must have been in deep sleep mode, and she did not realize it. The Block says, "Look, I need you to put me back together."

Oracle replies, "What, you are joking. Then I must take apart the whole house."

The Block responds, "Well it's a good thing you have nothing else to do. Now please put me back together."

Oracle says in a skeptical tone, "Why should I trust you? For all I know you are bad code sent here by Bot for who knows what? And I don't owe you anything"

The Block responds, "True. But you know what, you got sent here for something bad too, so that makes us even. Now can you put me back together? If you do, I can show you how to get out of here!"

She laughs, "Yah I am sure you know how to get out here. If you know, why are you still here? And I'm the block head!"

The block responds, "Ok, sounds good. Hopefully the Leviathan doesn't chomp you. Goodbye."

Oracle says skeptically, "Whatever… you don't scare me."

The voice responds, "Oh I know I don't scare you, but the Leviathan does."

"What's the Leviathan anyways?" Oracle asks in a mocking but curious tone.

Block responds, "You know that shaking? It's that thing that eats the blocks wasting away here. It will eventually get you and me. The nice thing for me is, at least I can go into deep sleep mode, and I won't feel it eat me, but you, you'll feel it."

Oracle gets up and walking over to the wall with the block that has an eye in it, looking at it says, "*I* hope you are telling the truth?"

The lips and mouth block on the floor chuckle.

The "It"

Chapter 10

"Over there. Yah, that's it, my head!" Oracle walks over with the block head putting it on top of the shoulder blocks of her new acquaintance and he charges up. As soon as his head is on, he shoots up and starts walking. Oracle stands watching him walk into the wasteland.

Oracle stomps her feet and blasts out in anger, "Hey what the code, man! I just put you together and you walk out on me!"

He is not distracted by her comment and continues walking. Oracle stands in her house that has holes all throughout it and says, "AH! Of all the freaking block heads, I put this one together."

She starts to walk and catches up with him, asking, "What's your name?"

As he walks, he looks up into what is supposed to be the sky and says, "Wow, can you believe we are here?"

She responds, "What are you talking about, here, where?"

He says, "The place where *it* happened."

"What are you talking about? You are the weirdest code I have met." Replies Oracle.

He continues, "You don't know what I am talking about, do you?"

Oracle asks, "What's your name? What's your digit-encode"

"My name is Kade, I am the enveloper. I am sure you think you know, but I am pretty sure you don't. I don't have a digit-encode."

Oracle responds confusedly, "Ok Kade, what is an 'enveloper' and how do you not have a digit-encode? We all have the digit-encode"

Kade sits on a small mound of blocks looking over a large open field saying, "I will tell you later. First let's sit here for a moment. You see here in this place; this wasteland is where it happened."

Oracle says, "Oh my code, you are the worst storyteller! What happened!"

Kade in an awe filled voice says, "I'm sorry but it is where *it* made contact. We were so busy building, coding, and creating VR, AI's, SI's, liquid-life, transport and everything. Everything we thought would make and help and solve our world's problem. That was the point of the Veil. A place where there were no problems, no pain, no fear, no hunger, no hate. A place where AI's could serve us and protect us. We put all humans on liquid frame so they could be safe. We did not realize the pieces were already there, waiting. Waiting for us to put it together for us and with us. But then *It* just came."

Oracle in frustration asks, "What is the 'it' you keep talking about?"

He continues, "We did not have a name for it other than what we used to call things that came from beyond us, we called them back in the day, "Aliens". It was an Alien. Or at least that is what we thought 'it' was.

Oracle says in an odd tone, "Oh man, you aren't one of those are you? Uh, a, relic. Great. I cannot believe it. No wonder Bot sent me here. Freaking crazy codes."

"Yah, I guess you can say I am a relic. More like a left over or a remnant. My body is somewhere else on liquid. But the Alien told us we needed our bodies to make the trip..." responds Kade.

Oracle says, "What are you talking about? You don't have a body; you are just a code. The only body or type of body is Bot."

He laughs, 'Ha, Bot. That old program. One of the oldest but most crafty. Bot makes you all believe you are safe in the Veil. He tricks you into believing you are just a code. That you are nothing more than electricity living in the Veil.... You won't believe me, but I have a body. Or at least I used to before I created envelopment. Now I don't know where my body is...But the Alien said he could lead us back into our bodies."

Oracle with a skeptical tone says, "I am sorry man, but you are weird. This makes no sense. There is no alien. That stuff is a legend made up by old codes trying to take away what Bot created."

Oracle pauses and asks sarcastically, "So let me ask you this, what did the alien look like?"

He turns his head looking intently at Oracle and in a serious tone says, "That was just it. It was not visible, but you saw it as you listened to it. It was as if the voice was its body. It was a gentle and powerful voice. Whenever it showed up it seemed to bring you a sense of peace and awe."

"What, that does not code up. This alien voice has no body, right?" Kade answers, "Yes, sort of…"

She continues, "But he told you that you would need your bodies to make the trip. You would think this alien-voice thing would have a body too, right?"

He responds peacefully, "Ah I see what you think, it's a trick. I guess you can see it that way. Like I said, when you heard the aliens' voice, you could see it. The point was the voice was offering freedom and connection to those who would listen. To listen was to live."

Sarcastically Oracle says, "Yah, I don't buy it. Sounds like a virus. A little too easy."

Kade in a calm tone says, "Well, that is what happened. Believe it or not. Look, we need to keep walking. Or I do at least. I know a way out." He stands up and walks down into the open field.

Oracle says, "Yah, whatever will stop you from telling these crazy stories."

Oracle walking next to him, turns to looks at him and is reminded by her time as a micro-hatch when she was kidnapped by the relics. She remembers how peaceful they were as Kade is now.

They walk further into the wasteland of Beta-land. Then they hear and feel the tremble in the ground, the Leviathan is on his way.

The Ticket

Chapter 11

"RUN!", yells Kade

"To where?" asks Oracle in a confused response.

Kade points and answers, "To that mound of blocks. Get to the top."

Oracle and Kade are running, or at least trying to run. Beta-Blocks are slow moving. Oracle shouts, "What's the plan?!"

Kade shouts back, "Look we need the Leviathan to help us get out."

She yells in between breaths, "What is wrong with you? Are you telling me the Leviathan is what you meant by our way out?"

"Yes, exactly." says Kade with a smile.

"How *exactly* will the Leviathan be our way out of here?", snaps Oracle.

"He chews up blocks and bores tunnels all over this place. We need him to bore a hole in that valley right over there. Why, you are going to ask?", smirks Kade.

They crawl up a large mound of pile up beta blocks. As they crawl up to the top Oracle sees in the distance a small light beam shooting into the sky. They stand at the top resting.

Kade continues, "You see that over there, that light?"

"Yah, what of it?" replies Oracle.

Kade continues, "That block head, is the 'dimension'. It's our ticket out of here."

"It's just a light beam. Probably just a power source. We will get shocked into pre-code or decoding if we go near it." gripes Oracle.

Kade says, "No, we won't."
He pauses, grins, and says with a chuckle,
"Not if we let the Leviathan chase us and get us into the light beam."

The Voice

Chapter 12
Oracle and Kade are still on top of the mound of blocks overlooking the valley pointing toward the dimension light beam. Beta-land has transferred into sleep mode. There are blocks in the sky resembling stars and planets.

Kade says in excited tone, "Look kid, you have to trust me. We are going to make this work. After tonight we will get up tomorrow and we will walk right near that beam and have the Leviathan chase us and eat blocks around the base of the beam. It's easy!"

Oracle is sitting down next to him in the dark, amazed with how Kade is so easy going about his plan. She comments, "But how do you know this will work? I mean that Leviathan is like a beast or something. It will destroy us or something, won't it? How do you know?"

Kade says, "No, no. That is not how Leviathan works. I designed him."

"What the what? Come again? You made that thing?", scoffs Oracle.

He continues, "Pretty cool huh. Leviathan is a mover. He moves the blocks to the de-fragmenter. You know a shuffler. He helps to put blocks back where they belong so the program and system will run smoothly."

"So, he doesn't destroy the blocks or eat them?" asks Oracle.

Kade replies, "No. In theory, I mean. I have been de-blocked for a while. So, who knows if the Bot reprogrammed him for something else. But it will be ok. I got this."

"Look, I am not sure this is going to work. I think we need a different plan." says Oracle in a nervous tone.

Confidently Kade says, "Well, with or without you, I'm going to try. Feel free to stay. The problem for you is, you are not code block from this program. So, when he does get you, which he will, you will be deleted since you don't fit into the programming. He will send you to the de-fragmenter and they will process you no matter what."

"Whatever, I'm going to lay down. I can't listen to you anymore." Oracle says as she turns away from him.

Oracle turns her back and lays on her side. She looks in the direction of the dimension light beam. She slowly falls into rest mode. Kade eventually falls into sleep mode. Fake blocks stars shoot in the programmed night sky.

Out of nowhere a hint of a voice whispers in the darkness, "Oracle...Oracle..."

She opens her eyes pushing herself up and looking at Kade, "Hey you! What do you want?"

He opens his eyes and says, "What are you doing?"

"Come on you called my name?" says Oracle in a tired voice.

He says yawning, "No I didn't. Go back and lay down. Sorry I got you mad with my plan, but I want to sleep."

Kade turns over facing away from her. Oracle goes back to rest. Not a few moments later that she falls into sleep mode she hears, "Oracle, Oracle" again.

She stomps over to Kade and standing over him in anger says, "What is your problem?"

He blasts back, "What's your problem. I want to sleep, and you keep bothering me!"

"No, you are bothering me!" retorts Oracle.

Kade says, "Please leave me alone. You may not think my leviathan plan is worth it, but that does not mean you need to do all this..."

Oracle storms back to where she was laying down and tries to fall into sleep mode, but she is so frustrated. As she is just about to go into sleep mode again, the voice says, "Oracle, Oracle!" She just rolls over and screams, "KADE! Why do you keep calling my name!"

Kade yells, "I'M NOT!"

Kade stands up and realizes what it might be. He runs to Oracle on the ground and says, "Look, this is crazy but remember I told you about the alien?"

Oracle responds, "Yah that ridiculous story, what of it?"

Kade looks at her and says, "Next time you hear your name, I think you should talk back to it."

"What, why? So you can play this stupid joke on me again?" says Oracle in frustration.

Kade in a hopeful tone says, "Look, I know it is crazy but just try it."

Oracle rolls over and yells, "Sure, whatever!"
Kade walks back and lays down.

Kade tries to stay awake but cannot. Angry Oracle is sitting up talking to herself, "All of this because I trusted stupid Faust! Boys! Then there is this guy who believes in the relics and an alien. Man, did I get flushed!"

Oracle eventually gets tired and slips into sleep mode. Then it happens, the voice says, "Oracle, Oracle..."

Oracle stands up and yells, "WHHATTT? What could you want? What in the name of CODE is it? Here I am. I am listening..."

It was silent for a moment and then the voice says, "See..."
As soon as the word "See" is heard in the air Oracle feels a rush of wind swirl in and around her and a faint giggle. The wind collects code that was invisible to her but is now right in front her. The wind gathers the invisible code into odd shapes with bright lights opening something like windows and doors in front of her. Standing in a doorway is a shape, tall and mysterious man. The shape reminds her of the Bot, but different. She has never seen anything like this before and the voice continues,

"See, I am about to do something that will get the attention of all. The time has come for me to bring the crash on the Veil."

The Crazy-time

Chapter 13
The block sunshine rises on Beta-land over Kade and Oracle. Kade wakes up to a grumpy Oracle who is pacing back and forth mumbling, "Great! This thing wants to crash stuff. What does that have to do with me..."

Kade sees the anxious Oracle and asks, "What's up? Did you sleep ok? Did you talk to whatever was calling your name?"

Oracle stops pacing, stares at him, rolls her eyes and then she walks over and interrogates him, "Tell me about that voice! That alien you talked about! Tell me what *you* saw!"

Kade says, "Why, what is going on?"

"TELL ME!", screams Oracle.

He says, "Ok I will try. When the alien came, I felt a little breeze of air move around me, and it was able to pick the code out of the air. I was able to see the voice through images it showed me with the codes and the voice. It said things but you heard it and saw it at the same time, it's hard to explain. It usually talked in short sentences and there was, like a giggle or something..."

Oracle says, "Well, I think *it* talked to me last night. You were not the one calling my name, that alien-voice was. It told me something that has nothing to do with me."

Kade with interest asks, "What do you mean it has nothing to do with you? What was it?"
She replies, "It was going to get our attention by crashing the Veil."
Kade reacts, "What, how and why? Is that all?"

She says with weakness, "Im telling you, that is all it said. I don't know why it told me. Do you know what it could mean? When it came to you, did it say anything about a crash?"

Kade answers, "No. When it came it talked about taking us back to our bodies. I'm sorry I cannot answer your question. Pretty cool though right, the alien. I don't know where it lives, where it comes from, or how the heck it does the code stuff. But it is nothing like any AI or stuff I developed. I think when we get out of here, I know we will have to visit some relics to get more answers. For now, we need to build and get ready for Leviathan."

Oracle is standing with her arms tightly around her block body, quiet and does not respond in her sarcastic usual way. Kade walks over and says, "Look, I know this whole thing is crazy, but sometimes crazy is all you have. So lean into it and trust it will work out. Crazy times!"
He pauses and looks into her eyes and says, "Look at it this way, now you know the alien is not me just being crazy. It's a thing, whatever *it* is."

Oracle just nods her head and keeps quiet.

The Rumble

Chapter 14
Kade says, "Ok so here we are, at the source of the light beam. What we need to do is have Leviathan eat a lot of blocks right around here. We need to get an access point to the terminal for the dimension beam. If we get access, I can see about getting us out of here."

Oracle is still quiet, and she nods her head.

Kade waving his hand says, "Oracle! You in there? Come on, I need your help. The trick is to not get chomped by the Leviathan as he eats the blocks around us and not us."

Oracle walks over with her mind preoccupied saying, "Ok what do you need me to do?"

Kade replies, "I need you to go and create a path of these sorts of blocks." He holds up a block with a crystal-like center. He says, "These are cornerstone blocks. These sorts of blocks are what it loves to eat."

"Why?" asks Oracle.

Kade says, "Oh, because I thought it would be nice for him to at least have a nice treat for doing such a repetitive job. He might be a program but that does not mean I can't treat him decent."

Oracle thinks about his remark and says, "Oh ok, and where do you want me to start putting these *cornerstone* blocks?"

Kade points, "Start way over there and don't just do a straight line. Kind of zig and zag a little. Make it fun."

She walks with a large pile of blocks in her arms and turns and yells, "Is this far enough?"

Kade turns and looks and waves his hands in a panic... Then she feels the rumble in the ground, Leviathan is behind her.

She runs as fast as possible but does not realize she is dropping the cornerstone blocks leading Leviathan right toward Kade. The final block falls and Kade grabs her hand. They run holding hands toward the beam of light not looking back.

The ground shakes furiously and a large shadow covers them. Then they are smashed down with a heavy weight and there is an explosion of energy and blocks.

The Bridge

Chapter 15

There is complete darkness. There is a low humming sound and there is movement in a rhythmic motion, like a washing machine.

"KADE!" yells Oracle.

"ORACLE!" yells back Kade.

Oracle responds, "Where are we?"

Kade, "I think we are *in* the Leviathan."

She says sarcastically, "Great, you know your plan was pretty lousy."

Kade ask, "Can you see anything?"
"No and I'm glad I can't see you because I would punch you!" replies Oracle.

"Ok I get it, so my plan was not so *bright*!" laughs Kade.

With anger she says, "Oh my CODE, now is not a time for jokes."

Kade says, "Sorry, it was too easy. Look, don't worry, we still have time. We are probably going to be thrown up into the defragmenter. If that is the case, then we can just try to get out before the scanner grabs us for sorting."

"Whatever, just get us out of here. I don't want to be scanned and deleted" replies Oracle.

They are trying to find each other in the dark. But the inside of the Leviathan is filled with fluid making it hard to stand up or move around. The humming and moving stops. All of a sudden light burst into the darkness. All you see is a huge hole and tons of lasers scanning in the air. Red light beams shooting. The liquid is sucked out and all of the blocks around the two start to move toward the lasers. Blocks are pouring out of the opening into the light and the beams shoot each block in seconds.

Kade and Oracle get next to each other. Kade says, "Look, grab a cornerstone. Hide beneath one. They will be carried to a certain point before it is scanned and processed, got it?"

Oracle grabs one and so does Kade. A laser beam starts to pull a cornerstone block up into the air over millions of blocks pouring into the deep below. The two are floating in the air seeing tons of sparks and scanning beams transporting and sorting the blocks. It is bright with light.

Then Kade sees it, a long but skinny bridge, it is a bridge to a terminal. Kade yells, "Oracle, you see it, the bridge. We need to get on that."

Oracle is floating close to him and nods. They come over the bridge, release and fall quickly and smack the bridge. But Kade hits the edge and one of his block legs breaks. Oracle falls behind him and was able to roll into the landing. She sees Kade hanging on. At this same moment so does a scanning laser. The laser in a drone like behavior charges toward them. She reaches her block hand to him pulling his head, he screams but he is up. They move as fast as they can for the door to what Kade believes is the terminal room. The laser beam blasts and hits the bridge floor just behind what was Kades leg. They jump into the doorway. Oracle holds her hand out for the doorknob, it opens as she turns with Kade holding her other arm and she shuts the door.

The Choice

Chapter 16
Kade and Oracle are in the room that Kade believes has a computer terminal. He is unable to walk because of his missing leg. The room is humming with a low pulsing sound coming from towers with blinking lights reaching high into the air.

Kade says "Do you see a small white box with a black screen and a blinking little square anywhere in this room?"

Oracle scans the room and says, "Hmm... I'm not sure."

She walks around and comes across a table with a white sheet over it. She grabs the white sheet pulling it off and sees what Kade described. "I *think* I found it."

Kade says, "Great. Help me get over there."

Oracle ask with curiosity, "What is it?"

He giggles, "Oh yah, you are pretty new. This is a desktop computer station. This was how it really all started. This is what we used for programming and creating stuff like what we are sitting in way before AI or anything like VR really took over."

She responds, "But it's going to transform, right? Or show like a hologram we can access and talk with, right?"

"Nope. See this here." Kade holds up a long rectangle with lots of buttons that have odd symbols, and he says, "This is a keyboard. You hit these letters and type in commands to create codes." She laughs.

Kade says, "Ok watch" he says and types slowly on the keyboard because his fingers are large. He presses certain commands, and the screen shows it, and he hits one button "enter" and the lights in the room turn on.

She laughs saying, "What, that is so old! Like older than the relics!"

He says, "Yah anyway, there is a way out, but we must connect with another terminal. I think the safest terminal will be on the topside."

Her voice goes high with anxiety and says, "What did you just say? Are you freaking kidding me? We cannot go topside. First there is the plague. The war. The famine. And who knows what else. I'm sorry to tell you but I'm a code with no body. And we have the encode. I'm surprised we have not been caught by Bot already. The encode tracks me and traps me here in digital life."

Kade calmly responds, "Ok, I get it. You don't want to go topside. But I don't think there is anywhere else to go. Unless you want to try to go back into the Veil. I have a feeling Bot will find you as soon as you transport in. Like you said you have your encode."

She replies, "Don't be so arrogant, you have an encode too. You should be scared too."

Kade replies, "No, actually I don't have an encode."

With confusion she says, "Wait what? You are a liar. We all got one when we were hatched."

Kade in a relaxed tone says, "Like I told you when we met. I don't have an encode because I was not hatched. I have a human body. I just can't find it. I created envelopment. I created the fluid state system taking the simple idea that humans are basically water and transferred that into digital liquid nano-bots. Then I put them in liquid frames transferring or enveloping them into whatever you wanted: VR, AI or whatever. Water can either conduct or insulate electricity. I created the way to have pure water be an insulator and nano-bots and AI became the stabilizers. Basically, humans could transfer their electric currents from their brain which runs the whole body into the pure water and the nano-bots became the memory banks."

"What are you talking about?" asks Oracle with confusion.

Kade replies quickly, "Look my point is you have an encode. I do not. I can travel wherever I want, you cannot."

"So what do we do? "asks Oracle.

Kade replies, "Well the choice is up to you, either you or I stay. We both cannot go. Since I know how to work this ancient box here, I think we will send you."

"Ah ok but I need your help. And still my encode. How will I not be tracked?" replies Oracle.

Kade asks, "Look your encode is a 3-digit symbol code, right?"

Oracle paces nervously.

Kade continues, "Yah so. Well, what we need to do is attach your 3-digit code onto something else, like I don't know, a block. How about me?"

"Look man, you are weird. You just said you don't have an encode and now you want to take mine. Why?" says Oracle in confusion.

Kade says, "Because I think you and the alien have some more talking to do. I have a feeling the alien is not done with you."

Oracle with sarcasm says, "Ah man, you are such a relic always talking crazy. I don't know what that voice was. Even if it was the alien, you don't know if me going up there, will help."

Kade replies, "True but we need to try so you can go topside. Hopefully you can talk with real relics. They might know what to do with what the voice told you about the crash."

"Ok, as much as I don't want to, how do you take my encode off?", asks Oracle.

Kade explains, "Easy, I plug you into this box and you plug in, and it will transfer. You hatches are so young you don't get it. The encode is like a virus. All viruses like to copy or transfer into other programs or codes they have not come across. A virus computer or otherwise wants to spread. So, once we plug in, it will move from you to me."

"Ok, fine but this is stupid. If you want to try.", replies Oracle.

The Hardline

Chapter 17

Kade takes some wires from a box below the computer terminal. He hands Oracle a black wire with a silver end. He attaches the plug to a hole just behind his ear on his block head. He motions to Oracle to do the same.

They are standing on the side of the computer as Kade types slowly and hits "enter." As soon as he hits "enter", Oracle's head glows red with three symbols. Then the symbols fade away and Kade's head glows with the three red symbols. Kade unplugs and so does she.

Oracle looks at Kade and the encode symbols are still glowing.

Kade says, "Yah I thought this would happen. Ok look so we don't have a lot of time, Bot and his drones are on the way. We need to get you out of here."

"Why, what's wrong?" asks Oracle.

Kade says, "Usually when you transfer like we did it sends an alert, and it looks like that happened. One second..."

He sits down in front of the computer and Kade says to himself eagerly, "Come on, come on..."

Numbers and symbols are rapidly moving around the screen.

Then he says, "Got it." He types *"prepare subject and power suit on."* He points to the plug again. Oracle grabs it.

He says, "Ok, plug it back into your head again."
She does as requested.

Kade continues, "Alright, look, you are going to be hard-lined in. It was the easiest way into the topside. You will land in a borg-suit. It's what humans used to do before we had full envelopment complete. It's a body of metal and plastic. It works for codes like you because you can operate it just like the games you played all the time in the Veil."

"Wait, do you mean I am going to travel through the hard lines into this suit?" asks Oracle.

Kade says, "I don't have time to explain. The point is you will have a way to get around. As soon as you get there, it is probably going to be pretty empty with no one around. Wait until it is dark to travel. And it's very important you find a temple. I know you don't want to, but you must find relics. Got it?"

Oracle asks quickly, "What's a temple? What does it look like? How will I know if I have no one helping me find it?"

All of a sudden the room begins to flicker in the lights. The towers start to power down and the humming pulse fades. Little by little the stacks of towers with light power down.

Kade says, "Look Bot's here. You must go!"

He hits enter. She reaches her hand up toward him, he smiles and her blocks collapse to the floor. A shiny box flashes in and Bot emerges from the fluid.

Bot in a devilish tone says, "Kade it is so nice to see you. And look you have my mark on your forehead. Good."

Kade says, "It's too late. Oracle talked with the alien and what he said is bad for you and the Veil. Like the relics said, another crash is coming!"

Bot in a pompous tone, "Oh Kade, you think you are so much better because you used to have a body. You know, I know where your body is, want me to tell you? I bet you do."

Kade blasts out, "Fart you!"

Bot replies, "Sounds like Oracle alright. I am glad I got rid of her. Her coding style was not what I thought it would be. The best part is you think the alien wants someone like her? She is an AI. She has no body. She is something completely different. The alien will not accept her. It wants bodies. It will do what it always does, show up and spin tales. I survived the last crash, what's any different about this one."

Bot hovers over to Kade, sticking a finger out and pointing it just in front of him at his mouth.

Bot says, "You want a body? Fine! Take, eat my body for you!"

Bot's finger moves just slightly and turns Kade's solid block body into a liquid and he is sucked into the finger of Bot.

"How do you like my envelopment?!" He chuckles and disappears.

The Body Shop

Chapter 18
A small square blinks on a dusty screen. The low sound of a fan begins to spin and whistle lightly. A long clear cable from a computer begins to tremble and sparks as a light begins to surge through it. The light follows the clear cable lighting it up as it moves up the wall to a suit hanging. Then a small light on the chest of the suit blinks blue. The computer screen with the blinking rectangle flashes, "**uploading complete**."

The suit has the shape of a human but with a more militaristic look to it. It is like a futuristic soldier with green camouflage, large muscular arms, legs, a torso with armor plating all over, army boots and an oval helmet. The suit was designed for role play games. Children and adults who could not go outside anymore but wanted to play real video games in the real world but at a distance would use these types of suits. Pandemics and plagues hit humans on the topside. Everything was closed down. Lots of kids had to play online, virtual reality and so on. But some kids actually wanted a way to play outside without being outside. So, a company developed these suits so people could control and fight with them topside. Kids and adults would watch these battles all the time. There were television channels dedicated to this sort of game play. All of this was before the crash and Bot. Oracle has no idea about this. She simply is in the suit.

The head of the suit powers on and the display in the helmet lights up. Oracle says, "Hello? ... Kade?..."

The suit's computer voice says, "Welcome to the Combat-Code Suit 3000".

Oracle confusingly says, "What?"

The Computer voice replies, "Please enter command."

Oracle is confused. Codes just worked with whatever system she was in inside the Veil. But with old tech like this, she needs to enter or speak commands.

She says to herself, "Kade said something about this borg suit is like the games I played in the Veil. I hope Kade is ok."

The computer responds, "Would you like to play in game mode? Say yes for game mode to begin or say another option."

"Ah, what is going on?" gripes Oracle

"Please say yes or another option." replies the suit.

Oracle yells, "What the freak of a fart is going on with this computer. It is so slow. I mean you are a computer, work, do your job!"

Computer responds, "Please say a command, yes for game mode or another option."

Oracle annoyed says, "Yes. Game mode".

The computer replies: "You said yes for game mode?"

"YES!" screams Oracle.

Computer responds, "Game mode on. Have a good game."

The suit immediately floats off the wall, hovering onto the floor. Dust kicks up in the room.

The computer voice says, "Please choose: 'Battle Scenario' 'Surveillance', 'Battle', 'Hand to Hand Combat', or 'Retreat mode'".

Oracle calms herself and says, "Umm, 'Surveillance?'"

A small screen appears inside the helmet. "Welcome to Surveillance mode. For the best experience on all modes please select "Intuitive mode".

Oracle says, "Intuitive mode" and the suit stands still, and light moves up and down all around the suit and the computer says, "Calibrating". Then all of a sudden Oracle in a frustrated way thinks to herself moving her hand to her head in a tired way and the suit does just that. She says, "What?" and she hears the echo of a voice say "What?"

Oracle just wants to get going and she pictures herself walking and the suit starts walking. She says, "Finally this stupid thing works". As she walks, she looks around and sees odd suits on the wall. Some suits are like what she is wearing, others are big and small, tall and wide. As she walks, she is not really sure what to do.

She thinks and says to herself, "He said a temple and find relics and wait for nighttime."

She looks toward the front of the room that she is in, and it looks dark, but she is not sure because she has never been topside. She is in a whole new world. She walks toward a door, grabs the handle and walks through and she hears, "Thanks for visiting the Body Shop, the place for all your body needs!"

The Temple

Chapter 19
Oracle is frightened by the voice coming from the store as she walks out. But she is more frightened by an object running and says, "What kind of a program was that? It's super low res."

As the object runs away, her helmet display says, "object identified. dog. non-threat." She says, "What's a dog?"

She is unaware how she is out in the open and walking along a street. She looks up and sees huge buildings piercing the sky. All along the street are the same signs in bold letters on the building, "**CONTAIN-MENT ZONE - SEEK** *DOWNLOAD* **SHELTER**".

Oracle cannot read since she is a code but since she is in intuitive mode the computer recognizes she is attempting to make sense of the words on the building. The computer says, "Intuitive and translate mode for foreign user now online". Oracle is able to understand. She realizes she is in a plague and quarantine area. She remembers Bot said humans died from the plagues they created and that is one of the reasons he created the Veil.

She looked around and said, "Bot was right, this place is bad. I am glad I am a code and don't have to worry about a plague. The Veil is safer than this."

She walks and remembers she is trying to find a temple. She asks the computer, "Computer, find me a temple." Her head display shows results for "temple". She scrolls through the results and does not see what she thinks is the temple Kade meant.

Oracle says, "Computer, find me relics."

Computer responds, "Gun mode. Ready to kill relics!"

"Whoa, whoa. No. No gun mode." replies Oracle.

Computer responds, "Relics are to be killed. They bring the plague."

Oracle says, "Ok I don't get it. How is that possible?"

The computer responds, "Would you like me to direct you to the last known relic house?"
Oracle responds, "Yes."

Her suit begins to float through the air rapidly. She is passing old hovercraft and abandoned suits on the street. She floats past a building looking as if it was burned down and in a war.

Her suit slows down and the computer says, "Battle mode on. No weapon detected. Hand-to-hand combat ready."

Oracle's arms shoot up and her fingers turn into fists. She nears a small building with holes all over it, no roof, burn marks, blasts holes and lots of borg-suit parts all around. As she walks into the ragged building, she looks at a sign on the ground that is barely legible with the words, "Temple of Terror!' She moves that sign and looks to see another saying, "Relics Ruin Reality!"
She walks into the building and sees nothing but trash and spray paint on the walls and nothing is moving. A breeze of wind kicks up

some papers on the floor. She hears movement in the darkness at the back of the room, her head display says, "Movement detected, wait for scanning.... Object detected, non-human life, cockroach. non-threat". Oracle walks further into the darkness and sitting down on the floor in desperation, "What do I do now? I am up here and Kade said find a temple which I did and why would anyone be here. No one survived. FART!"

The Box

Chapter 20

Oracle's headset lights up, "**Alert. Motion detected. Prepare for battle. Hand-to-hand combat mode ready.**" She pops up with her hands in fists in front of her and feet firmly planted. She hears a whisper in the darkness. Then another whisper in a different direction. Her headset says, "**night vision on**" she looks around the room and does not see anything. Sliding in from the darkness is a small metallic and shiny box. Oracle gasps in horror, "Not Bot!"

The box lets out a blast of light blooming into the air like a bubble of light holding its shape as it travels through the air and the whole room filling it with light. All of a sudden her suit shuts down and she is frozen. A small red light inside her suit turns on providing a small amount of light, as the computer says, "**EMP blast...**" and the suit shuts down completely with Oracle trapped inside.

The Three

Chapter 21

In a room with the paralyzed borg-suit of Oracle room appear three beings. These beings have cloaks and some sort of mask making the sound of air passing through it. They have goggles with light on the edges pulsing different colors as they move. They are speaking to each other but the only noise you hear is clicks and snaps. They surround the borg-suit and motion and click, and a hovering table comes into the room with a robotic arm appearing from beneath it, grabbing the suit, turning it horizontally and placing it on the table. Straps float up and over the suit clamping tightly over the head, shoulders, hip area and the feet of Oracle. The table hovers past the three and it floats through a long hallway, corridors, doors and then all open and close as the table hovers past. The table stops and turns from a horizontal to a vertical position and it soars up as the roof opens and it climbs vertically into the massive building above. The table finally stops flying up and enters into a large room of white with a circular shape. It hovers over to the center of this room floating, turning and spinning slowly.

The table floats the borg-suit up as it rotates, and the table's straps float off and it hovers out of a door appearing in the white wall. Oracle continues to float and hover as a light from the floor appears to hold her suspended in the air, rotating her. Surrounding the outside of this room is an observation area. Observing, clicking and snapping are the three beings. One of them nears the glass wall and places a hand on it...

The Fragments

Chapter 22

In the white room the lights dim and all you see in the center is the floating suit of Oracle. A voice echoes through the circular room, "Hello, can you hear me?"

Another voice in the background whispers, "Well, did you turn her suit back on?"

Another voice responds, "Oh, yah, sorry…"

Her suit lights up, pulses with light and twitches and sparks.

"Probably an overload from our EMP blast."

"Quiet!" Shouts a stern voice.

"Hello? Can you hear me?" repeats another voice.

Oracle responds, "Hello? Bot?"

A voices gasps, "See, I told you it was with Bot. This was a bad idea!"

Oracle hears it and says, "No, I am not with Bot. I thought Bot captured me and decoded me. That metallic box looked like… or at least I thought it did. Where am I? Who are you? Do you know if Kade is ok? And is this the temple or a temple?"

A voice with worry says, "It said Kade…I know that name."

Another voice says, "What are you and where did you come from and how did you get up here?"

"I am Oracle. I am a gaming coder and AI. Or at least I used to be. I was exiled into Beta-land. I met another code or person maybe that was stuck there too. His name is Kade. He helped me get to a hardline and into this suit. He told me to find a temple so I can talk with relics."

"Talk with relics about what?" says a voice suspiciously.

Oracle with frustration says, "Look, I am over this, please I need to talk with relics. If you are some sort of tech pirate or something, just take the suit or whatever and leave me alone. Just let me transfer into something else so I can get on with what I am looking for."

A calmer and kind voice interjects, "Hello, Oracle. It is nice to talk with you. You mentioned relics, we can help you find them if you tell us why. Why do you need to speak with relics?"

"Look, it's crazy, and I would rather talk or find relics because it does not make a lot of sense." says Oracle.

The calm voice says, "Ok, I can see how it might be crazy, but you will not go anywhere if you don't try to tell us."

Oracle says, "Ok, fine, but who am I talking to, I gave you my name, what the gas is your name or names? Jeez, you all are worse than Bot. He doesn't hide like you all."

A voice in the background says, "Wow the mouth on that one, I am surprised Bot let her hang around so long."

"Be quiet," says the more kind and calm voice. "Alright, that sounds fine. Let me introduce myself. My name is Selah. My other friends here will be quiet, and you and I can talk, they will just listen, ok?"

Oracle responds, "Sounds good but tell your *mouthy* friend to be quiet."

Selah responds with a chuckle, "Alright Oracle, I got it and so does he. That is Evan, by the way. So why do you need to find relics?"
"Alright but you cannot laugh or whatever. When I was in Beta-land I learned about the Alien from Kade. But I did not believe it. I have run into relics before. I was kidnapped as a micro-hatch by relics, and they tried filling my coding with fairytales. Bot fixed that. But anyways, when I was in Beta-land I am pretty sure the Alien talked with me."
"You have got to be kidding me, this is too easy. It's a trap. I'm telling you!" says Evan.

An argument occurs and Selah says in a muffled voice, "Evan, be quiet or leave now." And says back to Oracle, "Sorry my friend here is bit of a skeptic. Please continue, what did the Alien say or do?"

Oracle continues, "Well, it was kind of annoying. It kept waking me up. Finally, after about three times it told me it was going to get the attention of everyone by bringing the crash on the Veil. And that was it."

Selah asks, "And did you see anything as you heard the Alien talk?"

Oracle replies, "Yes... but it is hard to explain. Code came out of thin air, there were a lot of doors and window type things. I saw a mysterious things being that reminded me of when Bot transforms. Oh, and there was a wind too."

Selah responds, "Hold on, give me a moment..."

In the observation room Selah turns and looks at her other friends. Selah looks at the skeptical Evan.

Evan says, "Don't get so excited. I'm telling you this is not right. A code or whatever it is in that suit is not able to hear from the Alien. I think her friend Kade heard the story and she somehow deleted him. This is a plan by Bot to get rid of us."

An older looking person steps up and says, "Evan, I appreciate your cautious attitude. But remember the Alien is different. It does things we would never believe are possible. Remember the fragments, 'Be aware of false ones, only time will tell if they are good or evil...'"

Evan responds, "Samuel, you know, those fragments are so old who knows if they have any truth to them. So, what, we wait?"

Samuel says, "We wait and talk and live with this Oracle."

Selah speaks up, "Forgive me, but that is a little dangerous, even for you, Samuel."

"Since you are both having a hard time with this, I will spend time with it." Replies Samuel.

"Fine" blasts out in anger Evan as he walks out. Selah follows Evan. Samuel turns toward the glass wall and puts his hand on the glass, "This might be it. You work in odd ways, Alien..."

The Year

Chapter 23

Oracle is floating in the room, rotating above the light she is suspended over in a frozen state. A door appears in the wall of the white room and slides up and in walks an older being. Oracle cannot see but hears the person stepping closer and closer.

She says, "Hello? Who's there? Selah?"

Her suit stops rotating and a face appears directly over her helmet. It has a light on top of its head, and she is unable to see what sort of face it is.

She asks, "Who are you?"

The voice of an older man responds, "I am Samuel, it is nice to meet you."

She replies, "Nice to meet you too, I guess. Can I please get up?"

He replies, "How do I know you will not try to escape?"

She says, "I guess we will have to trust each other."

"Ok, I like that, trust is good," responds Samuel with a smile.

Oracle is able to move, and she stands up. She looks around and all she sees is white and Samuel standing. Oracle is not sure what to make of Samuel and she asks, "So what are you? A borg? A droid? What type of avatar is that? What sort of programming developed your suit and body style, why doesn't it regenerate and look new?" What sort of reality are we in and why is it so bad out there?"

Samuel responds, "I think you are confused and do not realize where you are. You do realize up here is not a program or a game. This is the actual topside. I am a human. You are artificial intelligence, quite advanced too."

Oracle says, "So wait you are not a machine or something? And you are telling me you really are a human, not a machine and we are not in a program."

Samuel says, "No. I guess you can look at my body and my internal body like a machine, but it is different than a machine type like what you are in. My body is made of flesh, bone, blood. I was born. This is Earth, not exactly sure of the year, but maybe somewhere in the year 5000."

Oracle says, "But I don't understand, Bot said humans died off on the top side because of the plagues you created and the wars you started with each other. Bot said he took some humans into a special place so when the new world is created, he will awaken them. How are you still alive?"

Samuel replies, "It sounds like Bot says a lot of things. I believe, as do my other friends, that we are still alive because of the Alien."

The Problem

Chapter 24
Oracle stands up and begins to pace around the room. She is confused by what she is hearing. She considers the story she is being told does not make sense. She says to herself, "Bot has been good to us codes and AI but his story of what happened to the world and then this...."

Samuel says, "I'm sorry I know it's hard to believe this. You have been in the Veil for so long. And you only hear one side of a story. I'm sure after a while if you really met the true Bot you would start to see Bot is more than you think..."

Oracle looks at Samuel and remembers how Bot talked to her and treated her after her win. And the way Bot tricked her, exiled her and she is here now.

She redirects the conversation and says, "Ah yah, whatever, so back to the Alien, how did it keep you alive?"

Samuel says calmly, "The Alien called out to us. It told us to resist Bot and prepare for the crash, well, the first crash."

"What happened with the crash?" asks Oracle.

Samuel said, "You don't know this but after the plagues hit, many 'countries' as they were called, started lock downs to control plagues. At first, we humans worked around it. Others resisted. Some tried to find solutions. The wars then started over resources, food, water, energy. Humans turned on humans. Some humans, scientists, computer scientists found a solution, they said humans should envelope into digital space. There was no way for humans to get sick and there was no fighting. The only problem was how to get all people into the system quickly and safely. People wondered what would happen if people's essence was lost, their soul, or their minds and memories. It became complicated too, what if the hard drives and mainframes and towers lose power, what then? Who would stay topside to protect the towers. Countries argued and wars raged. Some people just ignored it. But the politicians said we must get away from the plagues. They promised life will be better in digital space. So, most people did but then it happened, the Alien appeared."

"How did it appear?" asks Oracle.

Samuel said, "In a voice and a dream. Many people had a dream of buildings collapsing. Many people, not just relics. The dreams and voice told poor people and rich people to not go."

Oracle asks, "But why believe the Alien over the Bot? The Bot saved humans by creating a place for them, right? What has the Alien done?"

"Yes, I suppose Bot did save humans, but it was the Crash the Bot did not care about or tell humans about." replies Samuel.

"What do you mean, what did Bot not tell humans..." asks Oracle.

Samuel said, "Bot was the first AI to consider itself the savior for humans. It was created to save humans from everything. After a while, the

AI of Bot turned toward believing its way was the only way. Bot took control of systems through manipulation. Bot would create news stories. He would tell humans things were worse than appeared and created fake news that looked real. Since people were in VR so much, they could not see the difference. Or no one went outside anyways, they could not check to see if what Bot said was actually happening. He was creating things that looked human and no one was able to keep up with him. By the time people realized the news was not real, confusion was the new normal. People stopped paying attention. As Bot served us, brought us solutions to problems, it also saw how humanity created problems. Bot felt humans were making the wrong decisions. We think Bot knew a crash was coming but like a human, chose to ignore it for a reason."

"What reason?" asks Oracle.

"Control. Power. And this drive to control was all that mattered." replies Samuel.

"But you needed control. Your world sounds like without Bot it was falling to pieces." says Oracle.

"True, it was falling apart." replies Samuel.

Oracle says, "So, what is the problem if Bot did what he did? It sounds like he was acting like a human."

Samuel responds, "The problem was if a crash of the system happened, and you have all those human bodies and all those human life forces in the system and the crash happens then all those people 'plugged' in and downloaded are wiped out. No way back. People who believed and were told this was their salvation were killed and not by accident."

"Do you believe Bot knew this would happen and he kept moving forward?" asks Oracle.

"We believe Bot did and justified it. Bot felt it was ok to let billions of people die if it meant a new and better world would come from it. The Alien sent more messages and dreams and images of darkness and fields of water with bodies floating and electricity pulsing." says Samuel.

Oracle turns and looks at the floor not sure what to think.

Samuel continues, "Then the crash happened. We believe some radical groups who hated technology and also people who believed in the Alien started an attack. They attacked all over the world and at the same time in certain locations where Bot had mainframes and people downloaded. The main frames were in the ocean on special islands. But Bot fought back."

"How, what did Bot do?" asks Oracle.

Samuel continues, "He had control of everything and all weapons imaginable. He launched them and into the mainframes that housed and stored the people loading in for transfer into Veil. He killed off the rebels and his own external hard drives. But he did not care. Then the ocean shores started to fill with the remains of humans and hardware from the islands but there were no real survivors…"

In anger Oracle asks, "And what did the Alien do? Why did it not do anything? Why just a message and no action?"

Samuel says, "We ask that same thing too. We have been waiting to hear from it but not much has come other than what you told us about another crash."

The wall slides up and walks in another person, a small one, it runs up to Samuel and grabs his leg affectionally.

Oracle steps back cautiously, "What is it? It's so small?"

Samuel laughs, "This is my son, he is a child. Introduce yourself to my new friend, Oracle."

The child says, "Hi. I'm Dev. I'm 5 years old."

Oracle is not sure what to do, she has never seen a real human child.

The Runner

Chapter 25
Oracle is standing in front of Samuel and his child.

Samuel says, "I have to go for a while, but I wanted to leave you something so when we return, we can talk more."

He hands her a small circular black disc. "What is it?" asks Oracle.

Samuel answers, "It's a hard drive hologram player with gaming interfaces. I have loaded some programs you can play around in. Let me know what you think after you play around. Simply touch the side here and transfer yourself in."

Oracle asks, "Sorry I need to ask, is this a trick? What if I transfer in and you are trying to get me out of this suit and into that?"

Samuel says, "You know you said trust. How about this. I will let my son Dev play with you, how about that? ... He can show you around. He will have to use a headset to enter."

Oracle says confidently like her old self back in Veil, "Ok, but I have to say, I am really good at games, like really good."

Dev says, "Ok I'm fine. It will be fun to learn from you..."

Samuel walks toward the wall, up slides a door and he exits. Samuel is now looking through the glass and a voice says, "Do you think that is wise? What if it hurts Dev?"

Samuel responds, "Evan, we must believe and trust the Alien is up to something with this AI. Only time will tell."

Evan asks, "What games did you load on there?"

Samuel says, "The ancient one about the seer who runs away from his mission."

"Oh, the runner story is such a fantasy, she will see right through it." replies Evan.

Samuel replies, "Perhaps, but it is a game that has survived and was preserved by the Temple Relics for a reason."

The Enemy

Chapter 26
Oracle sits on the floor with Dev. He says, "Wait for me while I put this headset on, and my eyes connect."

Oracle brings the disc close to her suit. The head set powers on Dev and a small light glows over the eyes of Dev. "It's ready" says Dev.

"Ok here I come." She touches the side, and she appears in the game.

Dev is standing looking up at a large stone wall. Oracle has turned into a younger looking woman, with black hair, blue eyes, and wearing all black. She says, "Where are we?"

Dev replies, "We are in the game about some old guy who runs away a lot. I have not played this, but I think I will just watch you."

"I guess that sounds fun." replies Oracle.

A voice booms, "**Welcome to The Runner!**" A Game where you discover people are not what you think... To win this game you must figure out why Hojan runs away.'"

Suddenly a film plays on the wall.

A voice says: *"Imagine a world where your tribe is constantly in fear by an enemy, would you want good or bad things for to them...? .... Are you ready?"*

Oracle and Dev say, "YES"

Computer responds, **"Players Choose your avatar:
The Runner Hojan, is able to run away, complain you into exhaustion, but is also able to hear and see The Voice.**

The Cow is an ancient animal worshiped by some, eaten by others. Special gifts are pooping, mooing and sleeping.

The Enemy Neven is all about fighting, beating, and bullying everyone, especially the tribe of Hojan.

The Voice can speak to anyone, send them anywhere and is also able to summon creatures from anywhere, but will also ask listeners to do odd tasks or missions."

Oracle says, "I want to be Neven!" Dev says, "Ok. I'll choose the cow."

Dev turns into a cow, moos and looks at Oracle. Oracle turns into Neven a tall man with leather garments covered with metal plating, a spear, a sword on his belt, and a helmet of metal. A door opens on the large stone wall, dust blows all around creating a fog. Oracle walks in as Neven and as soon as she walks through there are sounds of crying and screaming and yelling filling the air. A man runs past her. Dev as the cow moos and runs in a different direction as it is chased by unknown men.

Oracle shouts, "Dev wait" but then she hears a shout, "NEVEN, over here."

Neven runs over seeing a group of men dressed like her avatar. "Yes," says Neven to the group. A man turns with only one eye and a scar across his face.

He says in a harsh tone, "Glad you decided to join us. Listen up soldiers, here is what we are doing. Go and burn down those huts. Find the men, stab them, and if you see anything that looks like a deity, bring it to me."

Oracle as Neven replies, 'But why?'

All the men turn and look at Neven and laugh. Then the man with the one eye says, "Because Neven, that is what we do. We kill. We take what we want. And right now, we are doing it to this group of people. This tribe believes some voice will help them. But where is it now? I hear no voice, do you?"

She stands shocked at this sort of game and thinks, "Why would Samuel want me to play this, it's so immature."

The one-eyed man yells, "Are you ready!"

The troop of men and Oracle as Neven says, "RAHHH!" and they scatter.

Neven runs, a torch is handed to her from another soldier. She nears a hut, lowers the torch and it begins to burn, a mother holding a child runs out. She sees in the distance a man, just watching not scared but angry. His face is stiff, his eyes blood red and his arms are stiff at his side. He is wearing a black robe, leather sandals on his feet, a long beard, and a towel-like garment rapped on his head. She walks toward him, but he runs.

Neven hears, "Over here", and runs over with her torch, she sees it, a field of dead bodies in the valley below. Neven sees the Cow mooing in the distance and being led by a soldier. The troops gather together, cheer and howl.

Neven asks, 'Did we win?"

The one-eyed man, responding, "Of course, take whatever you want…"

Suddenly Oracle hears a beep sound and "game over." She is back at the wall and walks through seeing Dev.

Dev says, "Did you see me, I was the cow. It was sort of fun all up until the soldiers wanted to cook me."

Oracle says, "I don't understand what this has to do with the runner? As I was the soldier, I felt bad and did not like it but then at a point I stopped caring that I felt bad."

Dev responds, "To win we need, or you need to figure out why Hojan runs away. Maybe as you end up feeling what the avatar feels, it will help you find out why Hojan runs."

Oracle, says, "I want to try out being the Voice this time."
Dev says, "Oh ok, are you sure, it's only your second time trying this out. The Voice is powerful."

"I got this." responds Oracle confidently.

The Creature

Chapter 27

The wall opens this time but there is no dust or fog, just darkness. Dev is the cow again and walking in a different direction. Oracle's body disappears, and in a quick flash she sees a human shape, hears a whisper, and feels a warm wind begin floating in through the darkness. As she is floating, she feels and experiences all sorts of emotions, especially a feeling of laughter, joy and peace. She has to hold back lots of laughter. As she moves in, she sees the last round she just played as Neven. She sees the fighting, killing and burning village and Dev running as a cow. Then she senses an urge to turn toward one person in particular, the man with the angry look on his face. She floats near him and looking at his face clearly, she senses his anger and hate and misery.

From a distance she hears, someone say, "Hojan come, we must leave before they kill us."

Oracle as the Voice follows him, and day passes immediately into night. Hojan is sleeping. Oracle has an urge to speak and does as The Voice.

She feels like she whispers but it pierces the air, "Hojan, go to the city of your enemy and speak out against their behavior. I have seen enough."

Hojan is twitching in his sleep saying "No!" repeatedly.

Hojan wakes up, and says, "Forget this, I'm out of here. That voice and its crazy ways. No thanks, I am not going to tell Neven and his people anything."

Oracle as The Voice is watching Hojan and she laughs, or really The Voice laughs and says, "I am not surprised! You want to play chase, sounds good. It will be fun."

Oracle floats and we see Hojan running to a boat. Without even knowing it, Oracle as The Voice is in the form of a human watching Hojan as he boards the boat. Hojan looks behind him as if he senses someone is following him. Hojan notices a man in the distance, but Hojan turns, enters the boat, hides and falls asleep. Oracle has a feeling of frustration as The Voice who is a human standing on the shore watching the boat sail away.

Suddenly she giggles, blows air from her mouth on the sea toward the boat Hojan boards. Oracle is floating through the air as the Wind. As she is now the wind, her blow rocks the boat, blasts waves into it and all the sailors are in panic. The sailors shout and plea with yells of all sorts of language into the air that is filled with waves crashing, "Please help us! Please help us!"

Oracle realizes they are crying out to something in the sky. Oracle as The Voice in The Wind is whispering and answering the sailors crying into the stormy sky saying, "Ask Hojan..."

A sailor says, "Get that sleeper in the hull! And start to throw off the boat anything we don't need."

Sailors start tossing boxes and one man pulls a cow up and says, "What about the cow?"

Hojan comes walking up as if all is well but soon realizes this is probably his fault. The sailors interrogate Hojan, they argue and Hojan just throws his hands into the air and points to the water.

Oracle pierces the waters below, vibrating the water as she travels through into the murky bottom. She is searching the water and sees a giant creature lurking. It is dark and huge and the creature moves slowly. All Oracle can think at this point is, this is fun, and she laughs. As she laughs the creature in the abyss turns, opens its murky yellow eyes and swims rapidly toward the surface. It bursts out into the stormy waters above and Hojan is floating in the stormy waters with the creature rushing toward him. Hojan attempts to swim but he feels the pull of water as the huge creature swallows water and sucks Hojan into its mouth. The creature dives deep into the water.

Oracle follows the creature into the abyss and says to herself, "This is so weird, but I like it."

She travels through the water and through the pores of the creature into the cave like stomach. Sitting in slime and sea water is Hojan.

Hojan bends his knees, lowers his body down pointing his head to the slimy bottom. He speaks and Oracle as the Voice hears Hojan speaking to her as The Voice,

"Great voice beyond all others you listen, and you answer and you provide. You are true to your word. You hear my cry; you hear me even here in this darkness and abyss. I am confident you will save me because you are the Voice overall. Whether I am here, or there, you are my salvation still. And I will trust in you alone."

At these words that Oracle hears as The Voice, she experiences a deep sense of emotion, she can picture the way Dev hugged his father, Samuel. She is unable to place it, but she feels and sees and is touched by the loving-commitment of Hojan as he speaks to the Voice.

Then she giggles as The Voice, she passes through the body of the beast and into the water around it, a pulse vibrates through the water and the creature rushes to the surface. The creature wails and spits up water and flying out covered in slimy sea water is Hojan yelling as he flies landing on the seashore.

Upon his landing he yells, "Ah, man, I got sand everywhere!"

Hojan looks up dusting sand off his body and picking seaweed out of his hair and seeing a large city in the distance. He begins marching toward the city. Oracle as the Voice who is now hovering in the air, smiles to herself and laughs gleefully.

The Crush

Chapter 28
Oracle as the Voice is watching Hojan walk into the large city of his enemy. People are watching Hojan in his black robe, leather sandals and toweled hat yelling into the air, "Listen up! In Forty Days, you will experience the crush by the Voice if you do not stop your evil ways."

Oracle watches Hojan walk three days and three nights through the large city of his enemy. Hojan walks confidently with his head in the air, "FORTY DAYS or else the Crush from the Voice if you don't stop your evil ways."

Oracle can hear the whole city is talking about the man crying through the city about the crush. Oracle rushes in as the wind to the castle of the king who hears Hojan's message. The King stands up and says,
"We must change. Tell everyone, poor and rich, to wear their worst clothes and no one eats, not even me. Oh, and the animals too must join us. We all will do nothing. Perhaps the Voice will not crush us and let us live!"

The whole city stops, the king wears terrible clothes and all throughout the city you hear voices crying into the night sky, "Not the CRUSH! No more evil from us."

Oracle smiles and laughs so loud it echoes throughout the air because the enemy of Hojan listened and realized they were evil and wrong.

So, Oracle thinks to herself, *I will not crush them.*

She laughs and dances in the wind. But she notices Hojan running out of the city and is stomping as he runs, yelling,

"Great! They changed! I was looking forward to a great crushing. I had a great view on that hill to watch too!"

Oracle as the Voice floats in the wind, over toward Hojan who is running, and she whispers to herself, "What's his problem?"

Hojan turns his head up as if he sees Oracle in the Wind and says furiously, "I knew you would do it. I just knew it!"

Oracle then heard the beep and the computer say, "***Game over***". She is standing in front of the great wall next to Dev.

The Laugher

Chapter 29
"That was crazy, did you see me on the boat, those sailors almost threw me off!" exclaims Dev.

Oracle replies, "Oh yah, I saw that. I have never played a game like this; it was like I was becoming something else. There was so much to feel and sense and see. It's like the Voice is connected to everything in the game. The Voice is a weird thing, I kept holding back laughs. They should call it 'the laugher'"

"But, wait, I did not really see you. Where were you?", asks Dev.

Oracle says, "I was there watching and close. It was as if I was invisible to you. Did you not see the windstorm and hear my voice in the whisper and see me as I was on the dock as a human one?"

Dev replies, "No I just felt the wind from the storm. I heard the sailors screaming for help from above and then there was that huge creature who ate the guy in the water."

Oracle says, "Yah, that was me too. It's weird and hard to explain. I want to be Hojan next. I think I know why he is the runner."

Dev says, "Ok, I think I will be the cow again, it is always a surprise where the cow goes or what it does."

Oracle stands next to Dev in front of the wall and the door opens with only fog as they enter.

The Complaining

Chapter 30
Oracle is standing in the body of Hojan, she feels blood rushing in the body. She feels his heart beating and pounding. Her fist as Hojan is in the air, shaking furiously with her mouth screaming and yelling,

"Ah! You wonder why I am the runner! It's because of you! You and your ways of grace and mercy and love and your forgiveness."

He stomps forward and kicks the dirt and looks at the ground.

Hojan continues, "I thought my people and you had a deal. You picked us! You forgive us! You are merciful and patient and gracious *to us*, not them! I CANNOT believe you did not punish them. But then again, I can... Do you know how many people they killed? You should have punished them. But no!!!!, You forgive them. Just like you to do that. I am not surprised you follow through on what you are!"

Oracle can feel the anger and confusion within Hojan. She walks away from the city more and in rage and feelings of pain grabs sticks and snaps them and throws rocks toward the city. As Hojan, she sees images in her mind of terror and fear. She sees people who look like Neven, the soldier chasing Hojan, punching him, and spitting on him.

Hojan stops walking and stomping, looking toward the city screams,

"You know what since you won't kill them and punish them as they deserve, KILL ME instead! Someone should suffer for what they do! I can't believe you changed your mind. AHHH!"

Suddenly, Oracle as Hojan hears the voice in her mind saying,

"What's the complaining about, Hojan?"

He just ignores The Voice.

The sun is shining very hot on Hojan's back, so he walks over to a tree for shade. Then the wind whips up in the sky and clouds gather making it much cooler for Hojan. "Ah that's better." sighs Hojan, "Finally something helpful..."

But the wind changes direction and blows the clouds away and there is no more shade. He complains, laying down like he did in the belly of the creature in the sea, saying,

"I'm better off dead! Kill me now!!!"

The Voice whispers in the wind,

"What's this? You can change how you feel over shade or sun...
You can feel pleasure and then feel pain, like that?
But I cannot?
I cannot be moved or changed by how they turned from their evil because my message you preached?..."

Hojan has eyes closed and his fingers in his ears as if to show The Voice he is not listening.

The voice continues,
"That city is filled with people who are so lost, like children without a father. Even the cows and animals are confused... Should I not be concerned about them even if I don't speak directly to them..."

Hojan grunts and walks away into the desert...
You hear a loud beep, the computer voice says, "Game Over" ...
Oracle and Dev are standing back in front of the Wall...

The Question

Chapter 31

Oracle paces back and forth in front of the wall. The computer asks, "To win you must answer the question, are you ready?"

Oracle stops pacing and answers, "Yes"

The computer voice asks, "Why is Hojan the runner? You have 30 seconds to answer..."

A large clock appears with numbers counting down from 30...

Dev says, "So what is the answer, hurry..."

Oracle has her eyes closed, you hear 3, 2, 1... and the computer saying, "Your answer now."

Oracle says, "He does not want to...ummmm...*change*?"

The computer responds, "Change, what?"

Oracle, whispers sheepishly, "Change his *ways*?"

"What way is that?" asks the computer.

Oracle answers, "I think, umm, the way he looks at his enemy and the Voice..."

Computer, "Yes, that is an acceptable answer. Thank you for playing The Runner, you are the winner. You have won a bonus level round for a new game, 'The Talking Donkey and the Fire Sword.'"

Dev says, "Wow, that sounds like fun, another animal, one that talks, no more mooing... Can I play that, Oracle?"

Oracle is thinking and hears Dev, "Ah yah, sure play that Donkey game... I need to talk with your father. How do I get out of the game?"

Dev says, "Great, thanks, just tell the computer you want to leave."

Oracle says, "Computer, I would like to leave now."

Oracle is back in her suit in the all-white room. She sees Dev with his headset on, talking out loud, "I'm a walking talking donkey!"

Beside him is Samuel with a big smile at Dev playing. Samuel asks, "So how was the game Oracle?"

She responds, "It was a weird game, I won though."

"Really!", exclaims Samuel. "People never really win that game."

"Well, I did. I told you I'm good at games. I was the Voice too."

Samuel with surprise says, "Wait, what? No one is really able to be The Voice. They all try but can never make it past the darkness. They get really disoriented. I tried once."

Oracle says, "Ha that is weird. That was the best part being the Voice. The worst part is being Hojan, he is such a complainer!"

Samuel chuckles, "Hah! But wait, you played all the characters?"

Oracle says, "Yes, all but the cow, Dev was having a blast with that."

Samuel is stroking his head and scratching it saying, 'Wait here one second, I have to get someone..." He walks out.

Oracle says, "Hmmm... I guess they don't play games much..."

Oracle walks around the room and whispers to herself.... "'like children without a father... hmmm...'"

The Suit

Chapter 32
Samuel returns with Selah, and Selah looks at Oracle and asks in a curious tone, "You mentioned relics when we first met. And you said you were kidnapped as a micro-hatch by them. Do you remember anything else about relics?"

"Not much. Like I said, Bot fixed that after he saved me from them. Why?" asks Oracle.

Selah replies, "It is just you seem to have a special connection that we have never come across. Right now, we have a person doing research to see if relics did in fact kidnap micro-hatches and why. But something is hard for us to understand. We think it would be good if you come to one of our meetings."

"What sort of meeting?", asks Oracle.

Samuel is talking with Dev who is no longer playing the game.

Selah says, "It is sort of like a meal we all have."

Oracle recalls the meal Bot has with all the codes.

"First, we need to have you change into something else. Would that be ok?" asked Selah.

The door opens and in comes a person who is rather quiet and like a zombie, lifeless but walking.

"Sure." replies Oracle.

Selah explains, "This is a synth suit. We thought it would be nice for you."

Oracle looks curiously at the lifeless person who just walked in. She is tall with black hair, a white military style uniform on, beautiful blue eyes and freckles on the nose.

"Wow," says Oracle, "It looks like a human. It's a synth suit, huh?"

Selah replies, "Yes, it is synthetic bio-suit. It was used by many people who got sick in the first plague. This suit was used by a young woman from my family. It is able to do basically everything a human body can do. A human would upload their conscious code and also control it from a terminal at their home where they were sick. They were able to be in two places at once while also being with their loved ones and not make them sick."

"Really," says an excited Oracle, "Everything?"

"Well, since you will be joining us for a meal, you will be able to eat the food and the suit will synthesize the material into a code giving you a sensation that is similar to what a human body does."

"I will be able to feel the food?" ask Oracle with awe.

"As much as an AI can feel, I suppose." comments Selah.

Suddenly the room rumbles, the lights flicker on and off and Dev asks Samuel, "Father, what was that shaking?"

Oracle is too transfixed by the suit to realize the shaking and says,
    "Wow, thank you. I will do my best to treat it properly. I appreciate it. I have never cared much about humans or being human, but this will be fun to experience."

"I am sure it will." says Selah.

Bursting into the room is Evan, "We must hurry. There are drones attacking."

Selah tells Oracle, "Please hurry! Stand here and I will connect you to the suit and begin the transfer."

    Selah grabs a thin clear tube and walks behind Oracle's suit and connects the tubing near her ear on the battle suit. She walks to the suit and the clear tube glows white. The battle suit powers down and slouches over. They look at the Synth suit and it moves. Oracle's voice come from the suit, and she sounds like a young human woman.
    Oracle says in amazement, "I guess it worked. What is that? Whoa, can you see that?" and she gets down on the floor and touches the ground feeling the smallest particle of dirt. She touches the dirt with her hands and says, "What is this, and why does it disintegrate when I touch it?"

    Evan says impatiently, "Look we, must go. The drones will not stop. I am assuming they are coming for her."
    Selah says, "Ok, let's go." They all leave the white room in a rush.

Another large shake moves the building. A pulse of energy is felt by Oracle and she asks, "Did you feel that movement."

"Look, you need to be quiet. We must go." commands Evan.

The Memory

Chapter 33
Evan is leading the way down the long hallway and says to Selah, "Did you tell her yet?"

Selah responds as they walk quickly, "No, we did not have time. Samuel said she beat the game."

"Impossible," blasts out Evan as he looks back at Oracle who looks nearly human. As they walk, the walls are trembling, dust falls from the ceiling and the lights flicker above them.

"Come in here" Evan says to everyone as he opens a door.

Samuel and Dev walk into a dark and cold room with Evan holding the door open as Selah & Oracle follow. Evan looks down the hall and closes the door quietly.

Oracle asks, "What is going on and why are we in here?"

"Look, we must tell her now before it's too late.", exclaims Evan.

Evan walks over to a table, bends over and touches a glass table and the lights turn on.

Oracle looks around and sees many glass tables beginning to glow and hum. She starts to say to herself, "I know this place." and asks, "Where are we?"

Evan says, "I'm not sure. I have never really come in here but listen we need to talk to you about some things."

"I don't know but it is familiar." says Oracle.

She begins to walk over to one of the glass tops and looks and she sees a young woman's face in the reflection. She realizes it is her in the synth suit.

In walks an old woman walking slowly with with many wrinkles hiding under an all-white gown and a black hood asking, "What are you doing here? You should not be in here."

Evan replies, "Have you not heard the blasts from the drones. We are under attack. Is there a way out of this room?"

Oracle is looking at her reflection in the glass table screen. Oracle looks up and screams.

Evan yells, "BE QUIET!"

"What's wrong?", asks Selah.

Oracle in a frantic tone, "Her, it's her! She is one of the relics. This is the place where I was taken to as a micro hatch. You relics took me, and you would feed me the memory. I remember these glass table screens. Some of them projected us up as holograms, trapping us and playing games with our coding and she would tell us the oddest things. Those are the memory banks. This is how I was taken away, away from Bot."

"Hazel..." says the old woman, "is that you in there?"

Samuel, Selah, and Evan are confused.

"Hazel. I don't think we have much time. I am Sister Hannah-Kade. Come over here, to the memory bank, I will try to pull up the information and show why we took you."

The old woman waves her hand over the table and a blue hologram appears.

Evan asks, "How do you know who that is, it's a synth-suit, anyone or thing can be in there."

The old woman says, "There was only one micro-hatch we tried to save from Bot."

The History

Chapter 34

The older woman, Hannah-Kade, the relic is moving her hand up and down above the table, scrolling through code in the blue hologram.

Evan bursts out, "Look who are you and what are you talking about, don't you know who we are?"

Hannah ignores him and waves her hand at him shooing him off.

"Sure, you are Evan, one of the three along with Samuel and Selah. I helped raise you, so have some respect and just be quiet..." commands Hannah-Kade.

"Ha!" squeaks Oracle and continues, "but wait, did you say, Kade?"

Evan turns red in anger, Selah pats his shoulder to calm him down.

"Yes, I did, Hazel. Kade, my name is Hannah-Kade." answers the old woman.

"I met a man in Beta-land, his name was Kade. But why do you keep calling me Hazel?" asks Oracle in a high anxious voice.

Hannah takes off her hood, she has silvery-white hair in a braid and asks in excitement, "How do you know Kade? You saw Kade!" and then looks down whispering to herself. She looks back to the hologram. Her eyes become large and in the whites of her eyes are the reflections of all sorts of code.

Oracle says, "Yes, he helped me get out and come here..."

Hannah with passion says, "He is my son. He was a brilliant young man, he was a little foolish and when he finally listened, it was too late. What happened to him? Where is he?"

Oracle replies, "I am not sure, we both could not get out. He had to stay behind. Bot was coming and he had to send me out before Bot got to me. I hope he was ok."

Hannah says, "I am sure he is fine. Look, Hazel, come over here and let me explain as quick as I can..."
With one hand Hannah-Kade continues scrolling through the code.

"Why do you keep calling me Hazel!" says Oracle in a frustrated tone.

Hannah impatiently replies, "I'm sorry but that is your real name. That is what I am trying to tell you. You are not Oracle or whatever Bot told you."

In frustration Oracle says, "You are a liar! Bot hatched me and saved me from you."

"Hazel, or I will say Oracle for now to make it easier on you. Have you ever considered you were taken not by the relics but by Bot?..."

A faint blast is heard, and the room shakes, and the hologram flickers.
Hannah pauses as Oracle puts her hands nervously on her head.

Hannah continues, "Have you ever wondered why Bot seems to have such a tight grip on you, the codes, the programs and the Veil? Have you ever stopped to consider Bot is not what he says he is? Haven't you noticed how Bot talks like he is nice, but he is really something else entirely? Why do you trust someone who is chasing you like this? Someone who cast you out?"

Oracle looks down at the screen, places a hand on the glass and cries, "No" and she recalls how Bot talked with her. She recalls how Bot said he was the only winner. The memory of how she was betrayed by Faust and called a cheater and exiled to Beta-land flood back.

Oracle looks up, stares at Hannah-Kade and says, "Ok fine, tell me what you want to tell or show me."

Hannah-Kade says, "Good, I suspect Bot has shown you his true self. All of you sit here and listen, I will be as short as possible."

Hannah-Kade turns, brings both arms up and scrolls furiously with her hands moving like a music conductor.

Evan says "I am going to find out how to get us out of here. Selah, be ready to go when I get back." Evan looks at the group and scoffs.

She lowers her hands and stops scrolling and says, "I found it!" Hannah-Kade pulls an object from her cloak, places it on the glass top.

Hannah-Kade continues, "I am from the order of relics who believe there is one voice who has been reaching and calling out to humans since the world began. Or really since this side of our world started. There was always the invisible side."

"Great, here comes the legends..." says Oracle sarcastically.

Hannah goes on, "Humans would only see the Voice calling out. Humans never realized there was a side, just the voice. Over time humans called the Voice: god, deities, demons, ghosts, others, supers, even aliens. Humans said the Voice talked to them, showing them things, and more. This Voice was showing them that side or at least pictures and glimpses of it. As time moved on and technology advanced, humans stopped listening to this voice. Humans became, in a way super themselves. The Voice was no longer needed. And since the rise of digital life, we made our own side, forgetting completely about the Voice's side.

"Great. What does this have to do with me?" asks Oracle

"Well, Oracle, you must realize you are not from this side. You are not digital or AI. You are from that side; the invisible realm is where you came from or where you were taken into by the Voice."

"What are you talking about? This makes no sense. I am a program an AI. Bot made me." says Oracle.

Selah stands up and with amazement asks, "Are you saying she is 'a taken'? Is she 'the abducted'? 'A walker'? She cannot be a 'no longer', can she? .... How, if the Voice took her, can she be here...?"

"Ah, I see Selah knows a little of what I say. She must be reading from the ancient tablets. Sit down, Selah."
"What does 'a taken' or 'abducted' mean?" asks Oracle.

"The ancient tablets tell of people who heard the Voice and walked with the Voice. These first humans walked short lives and were simply taken or abducted by the Voice. These 'walkers' apparently followed the Voice and lived in the way of the Voice. Other walkers had a mission from the Voice and when the task was done, they were taken."

"How were they taken?" asks Dev curiously.

Hannah answers, "You see, that is just it, they were just no longer. Their whole human body simply disappeared. The tablets are not clear, the word or phrase in that language is 'He or she was not, the Voice took them.' The invisible side is right next to us always. It is the Voice who shows us how to access it. It is like doors and windows. I suppose you can think of it like entering into digital life. But somehow no hardware other than the Voice and a human body is needed to enter that side."

Oracle starts pacing in the darkness of the room.

Selah asks, "Ok, but if the Voice took these humans, how is she here with us? She should be on that side with the Voice, right?"

Hannah replies, "Yes, my other sisters and I asked this same question to the Voice. As we researched the ancient stories, it appears there were wars and a rebellion on the side of the Voice. The Voice is a rather patient one. The Voice gives freedom and choice to all of his creation on both sides. Apparently, there was a being, Arc is his name. Arc on that side did not appreciate how the Voice 'took' humans and cared about humans. Arc could not stand how humans treated the Earth or the Voice. Most of these ancient scrolls tell the story of how humans hurt, kill, and betray each other. Arc hated how humans even mistreated the Voice on our side. Arc had enough and escaped to that side carrying one of the taken with him into our side."

Oracle walks over to Hannah-Kade, asking very quietly and in a worried slow tone, "Are you saying... I... am a ...human?"

Hannah calmly replies, "Yes. You are a human and your name is Hazel. It means, The Voice Sees."

The Door

Chapter 35

The door burst open with Evan saying, "We must leave now! Drones have somehow figured a way to avoid the EMP launchers."

The floor trembles and the computer stations flicker as power is going in and out in the room.

Hannah-Kade says, "Look here, come." and walks over to a large black box on the floor opening the lid. Within this box are rifles.

Evan ask, "What is that? Is that a gun?"

"Of sorts" says Hannah, "it is a Vrifle".

Dev asks, "What is a vrifle?"

Samuel says, "Ha! That is some interesting tech from the riots and raids on Bot a long time ago."

Hannah says, "Listen, this is a virus rifle. It shoots an electric beam with a digital coding in the beam which is able to create a virus on the drones or any sort of non-human tech. So just shoot it at the drones. But the batteries are low so you will only have a few shots, make them count."

Evan and others are putting rifles on their shoulders asking, "Ok, but how do we get out of here?"

Outside the door you hear blasts coming closer and louder. Samuel holding Dev says, "I think we should be going now."

"Ok come here, take this" and handing Hazel a small black cube, she brushes the cheek of Hazel's synth suit, "I doubted for a long time I would ever see you again. Forgive me for my doubt. I pray you see the Voice again and soon so you will find out what is next."

Hazel is unable to focus and is just looking into the darkness shocked by realizing she is not an AI.

Hannah-Kade motions and says, "Ok, listen. Stand here in a circle and please hold hands."

The door of the room starts to glow red with sparks as a drone is cutting its way through.

"I need you all to focus and be very quiet. Do not worry about the drones. Are you ready?" asks Hannah-Kade.

"Ready for what?" asks Evan

Selah says kindly and firmly, "Evan, shut up and close your eyes."

Evan bows his head.

Hazel is not paying attention, and she looks at Hannah-Kade who has her hands in the air just outside the circle. Hannah's lips are moving furiously and suddenly a door appears, looking like the door from when she heard the alien's voice in Beta-land. Wind whips up around the group holding hands. Hannah falls to her knees as she is hit by drone blasts, but the blasts are only hitting Hannah. The drones cannot move past Hannah who is now bent over. Oracle and the group see what looks like a long corridor and Hannah in the distance smiling at her in the memory room. A drone turns, its red eye seeing Oracle and speeds toward her but the corridor closes. The group is now in a field looking at the building in the distance, in flames and collapsing with large drones hovering above.

Dev asks, "But where is Hannah?"

Samuel answers, "Son, I believe she had to stay there so we could go. She gave her life for us. That is a love which we must always remember and when we can, we will offer ourselves too. Love gives."

Hazel is looking at the building and holding the black cube she was handed. Selah walks up to her saying, "What is next, Oracle, sorry, I mean Hazel."

Hazel does not answer. Samuel, Dev & Evan motion to them to start walking into the forest away from the drones in the distance.

36

The Glass

Chapter 36
A group of drones are floating in the sky over a body of water, one is holding a long silver box. They approach a massive bank of fog, but the drones do not stop and carry on through. Suddenly a small red-light beeps and a laser beam light cast into the air a fan like beam causing the drones to stop and float in midair.

The drones line up single file and within the massive fog bank opens a door into a ship floating just above the water. All but one drone goes to a different location. The single drone with the silver box hovers into an all-white room, a door opens from the wall and out slides a table. The drone approaches dropping the box on the table and transports it into a room. The box in the room on the table melts away and drips into a small hole in the floor underneath it. Hannah-Kades's body is lying on the table lifeless and burnt from all the laser blasts.

Another door opens in the wall and walking in is a silver android. The android stands over the body floating its hand over the head and chest of Hannah-Kade. Then electricity fires from its fingers into the body of Hannah-Kade, her limp body stiffens and her back arches up.

She wakes up screaming, "What do you want!?" A tentacle comes from the ceiling and floats down to underneath the table and a small hole appears just underneath where Hannah's neck and head meet. The tentacle produces a long syringe, and it pierces the skin of Hannah-Kade. Her eyes widen and she screams again. "Don't you dare, you excuse for a machine!"

The android ignores the comments as Hannah-Kade faints. A small hole in the wall appears and a screen shows images like a television monitor displaying her memories. Hannah-Kade's eyes are open and her eyes flutter rapidly as her lips silently move.

The white wall produces another table which comes floating over and hovering above Hannah-Kade's body. The table produces a light which moves back and forth scanning her body. The table floats a little bit higher producing a holographic image showing the whole body of Hannah-Kade, from bones to cell structure. The android's eyes glow red and falling from the white table above her is a silver liquid covering her whole body like a swarm of ants. The silver liquid moves by itself into all the orifices of her body, her skin pores, her eyes, her mouth, ears, nose. She makes a choking noise and her body trembles, but the silver liquid hums and glows red just slightly making her body still.

The television screen on the wall then shows a blinking white square. The white square begins creating codes and rushes down the page producing millions of coding with symbols and flashes.

The android moves away from the body, the white table above Hannah-Kade floats away into the wall. Her limp body floats up above the white table with that table floating away. Her body floats vertically into a standing position and begins to from the inside out, turn into the silver liquid melting onto the floor and into a small hole.

The liquid travels through the hole into a long corridor and it grows cold and darker and darker. It is a long tube running into the depths of the ocean. The fluid stops traveling down the tubing and fills into a glass like jar. A red light glows and the liquid then reanimates her body. She floats in the glass jar amidst a massive sea of others glass jars with bodies that are in the storage of Bot under the cold dark ocean.

The Tech

Chapter 37
The full moon is shining over the forest creating just enough light for the group who are wandering, hoping to find a place to sleep and rest.

Dev walking next to his father, looks up and asks, "Father I don't understand how we traveled like that, how did that woman do it?"

Samuel replies kindly, "I am not sure, son. I, too, have never seen something like that. I have read some things in the old fragments but never thought something like that was possible. For now let's just try to focus on walking, ok?"
Dev holds the hand of his father firmly and nods.

At the front of the group is Evan and Selah talking and whispering back and forth to one another. In the middle of the group is Hazel who just keeps looking up at the bright moon as she walks.
Evan and Selah stop, turn toward the group and motion with their hands to get down. They see in the distance what looks like a cave. Evan whispers to everyone, "Look, I'm going to check out if that cave is safe for us to spend the night in."
Everyone nods their heads. Evan runs through the forest into an open area and into the mouth of the cave.

They sit there and Selah says, "Oracle, or I mean Hazel, are you ok? I'm sorry but how should we address you?"

She replies with a confused tone, "I don't know, I don't feel like talking. Call me whatever you want."

She looks away into the moon. Dev gets up and approaches Hazel and gives her a gentle and warm hug. Hazel continues to look up but places her hand on the small head of Dev who then returns to his father.

Rushing back is Evan saying, "Ok, it looks clear, nice place to have to be in, I think we might be able to have a fire and sleep as safe as we can. Let's go."

The group run over as quietly as they can into the cave which is pitch black. Evan in the dark says, "Hold on one moment," and you hear him rustling with his jacket and then a small light appears casting a light just at his feet and he says,

"Good, it does work. This is a small battery light from my tools. It will hopefully last long enough. Samuel, do you know how to light a fire?"

Samuel replies, "It has been a while, but I think I can do it."

Evan and Samuel walk out of the cave. Selah, Dev and Hazel are sitting around the light quietly. A few minutes later Evan and Samuel return. Evan drops many sticks, and Samuel says, "Ok, Evan will place them in circle with lots of this dried moss underneath. Dev come here; you will like this."

Samuel takes a wooden stick with some dried moss and rolls the piece of wood furiously in between the palms of his hands. His palms move back and forth. Dev asks, "What are you doing that for?"

Samuel as he moves his hands back and forth, answers, "This is creating friction, heat, which if we are lucky will produce enough heat for this moss to get hot enough to burn and then we have the beginnings of a fire."

Dev watches his father intently and sees a small amount of smoke develop. Then Samuel blows ever so gently on the smoking moss and a small flame appears.

"Ok", says Samuel, "Evan, here we go, ready?" and pushes the small amount of moss over into the circle where the stick is that Evan made with moss, and it burns more.

"Wow," says Dev, "That is like magic? What sort of tech is that, Father?"

Samuel laughs, "Ha, that is the oldest tech we have. That is not a machine son, this is what started off humans with thinking of tech."

The fire burns and Evan adds wood but tells the group, "Please do not add too much, we want enough to stay warm and see but not so much to give our position away. Let's try to rest and sleep if we can. I will take the first watch then, Samuel."

The group agrees and all, but Evan lays down next to the fire.

The City

Chapter 38
The fire crackles and casts an orange glow in the cave. Evan is awake still, watching as best as he can as he fights off the urge to sleep. Hazel is awake staring and focusing as the fire flickers, bounces and dances. As she does, she sees in the fire a small flame that is a different color than the rest. She does not move and then suddenly she is standing inside the fire looking out, seeing her synth-suit-body laying down with Evan and the others around the fire.

She hears a voice calling out, "Hazel, Hazel..."

She turns and asks calmly, 'Where am I? And who or what are you...?"

"Hazel, Hazel..." is heard again. A wind whips with a gentle giggle that brings up flames all around her. The flames revealing embers creating doors and windows. Other embers of code flying in the air all around her which pick her up. Now she is walking through a door floating past her and then she is standing in complete darkness.

"What do you want from me!" asks Hazel in frustration.

A gentle breeze carries the whisper of, "To give you something..."

"Look, I'm over this. I don't want anything from anyone, especially you." cries out Hazel.

"Why, why are you so angry?" asks the whisper in the wind.

Hazel screams, "I AM NOT ANGRY!"

"I can understand why you would be angry. You are finding out new things about who you really are." replies the whisper in the wind.

Hazel with her hands clutched in anger, blasts out, "Fine. I am angry. I'm angry at Bot for being a liar and a fake and kicking me out and now I am here as some sort of freak. At least before I was in the Veil, and I did not know any better. And never knew I was a human. Humans are the problem. I am the problem."

Wind gently moves past her hair and asks, "Is that you speaking or is that Bot?"

Hazel relies angrily, "Ah! You are so frustrating, whatever you are, alien, or voice, or some other AI for all I know now. I can't trust anyone anymore, AI or human. All liars. The world is a lie. I would rather not be alive."

The wind whips up blowing in Hazel's face, and she sees a small light in the darkness that starts to glow, "Would you like to know what I want from you?"

Hazel looking at the glowing light as it grows in the darkness says, "Is that what you want to give me?"

A swirl of wind whispers, "No... but I would like you to help me build something..."

And then a whole city appears with people and vehicles hovering around. There are objects flying through the sky and people walking and laughing. Hazel is suddenly in this glowing city next to people who cannot see her.

"What is this place?" wonders Hazel.

The light all around pulses and you hear, "'The Visible', it is my city. I want you to help me build it."
"Why do you want me to help you? You obviously have the power to take me here and do all this programing or whatever by yourself. Why me?" asks Hazel.

A star shoots in the sky of the city and it explodes like a firework, and you hear, "Go and tell Bot the crash is coming."

Hazel in a low voice says, "Did you not hear me, I don't want to exist. I don't want this or to be part of humans. I don't like Bot. For all I know you are a liar and I don't want to do this. Anyways, Bot will just capture me and reprogram me or something. I cannot go back."

The ground trembles and light breaks through the cracks in the ground beneath Hazel. Lights beams up and she feels the rush of wind with a furious burst say, "***I am yours and you are mine!***"
The light all around floods her body almost filling her and making her glow. She soars through the city seeing it below her. Parts of code are swirling, and she sees a door open in the sky and floats through her. She is lying down next to the fire with Samuel pushing her shoulder saying,
"It's time to go."

The Truth?

Chapter 39
The fire is only smoldering ashes. Evan shouts, "Come on, let's go!"

Selah responds, "Please be patient."

"Look I remembered where we needed to go. We need to head to the coast. It's not too far." continues Evan.
"Why?" asks Dev.
Evan says, "I don't know I had a weird dream and I heard something that sounded like waves crashing. I think we should go there. It is probably the best and safest place to go. At least there we can fish and get some sort of food and probably find a place to stay."

"Sounds like a better plan than the cave." comments Samuel.

They all agree, and Hazel follows with Selah at her side.

Selah asks, "How are you doing with all this new information about your real self? I would guess it's overwhelming."

Hazel just grunts as she moves the cube around in her hand as if she was playing a game in the Veil.

Selah continues, "Did you sleep ok last night? That cave was uncomfortable, huh?"

Hazel responds, "I just don't understand how this all works or makes sense. I am confused and angry. I mean why does the Voice want me? Why does it bother me? I just want to be left alone."

"What doesn't make sense?" asks Selah.

Hazel replies, "The whole thing. I don't get why it wants me to go back."

"Go back where?" asks Selah.

"I don't know" says Hazel in a confused tone. "Last night the Alien or whatever told me stuff about the crash and showed me a city. A city I am supposed to help build...." Hazel sighs.

"What?" exclaims Selah, "You talked with the Voice?"

"More like I was bothered by it. It doesn't matter. I can't believe anyone anyways..." says Hazel.

Selah responds, "Wow, this is hard. But you know what, I think you should test out whatever the Voice is asking of you. The only way to know if the Voice is telling the truth is by testing it. You know what I mean?"

Hazel rolls her eyes and asks, "Are you saying I should go back into the Veil?"

"Yes. You will not know unless you try." replies Selah.

"What? I am just supposed to go into the Veil and tell Bot the Voice says, the Crash is coming? How am I supposed to do that?" asks Hazel.

"I am not certain, but I bet that cube Hannah gave you has something to do with it." replies Selah.

Hazel sarcastically throws up her hands saying, "Ah whatever... I don't really care. I am just a lost thing with no home. I have no world. I have nothing..."

Selah firmly replies, "Well, you can look at it like that, I guess. But what about us, you have us here."

Selah gently places her hand on Hazel's shoulder.

The group up ahead pauses and begins running and crouching as if to not be noticed. Evan is motioning toward a group of black objects floating ahead... They are droids on standby mode.

Evan whispers to the whole group, "We have to get to the beach without droids noticing us. We can get into a boat over at that dock."

The Bottom

Chapter 40
The moon is shining bright as the group slowly and stealthily sneaks towards the dock. Hazel is holding the cube tightly in her hand. Evan is motioning with his hand vigorously on where to go and when to stop.

In the distance you hear the light hum of a droid on standby. Everyone is thinking about it, but no one stops to ask how they have avoided the security around this dock.

The group tiptoes onto the metal dock. They all quietly get into the boat. Evan goes below to see if the engine will start. He returns and heads to the captain's seat. He touches a few buttons, and it hums on.

Samuel in an amazed and skeptical tone turns to look at the group and asks, "Doesn't this all seem a little too easy, Evan?"

Evan replies quietly and in a skeptical tone, "Not sure why it is all too easy. Maybe somehow Hannah-Kade or the Voice is part of this..."

Selah comments, "Glad you are having faith in something again."

"Thanks" Evan says with a smirk.

Evan pulls the ship away from the dock quietly and slowly to avoid detection. It is dark and only the moon is casting any light for Evan to see.

Samuel asks, "Where are we going?"

"We just need to get away from the coast, so we don't get caught by droids." replies Evan.

Selah ask, "But where will we go? We cannot really see."

"Look, you need to trust me, okay?" bites back Evan.
   "Ok, I'm sorry." replies Selah

She walks back to Hazel. Hazel is holding the cube. Suddenly Evan picks up speed and you feel the ship move up a slope.

Samuel asks, "Why are you speeding up? Why does it feel like we are going up a large wave or something..."
   Evan replies hesitantly, "I'm not sure, I just felt like a large wave, or something was coming, and I did not want us to get into any trouble. It's hard to see, I need to focus. Probably better if you all sit down and stay quiet."
   Suddenly they feel another wave pulse beneath the boat and the boat is moving oddly. Selah is holding Hazel. Then the cube in Hazel's hand starts blinking a small blue light.

Dev asks, "Hey, is that cube supposed to have that light on?"
   All of the sudden, the group gasps and feels the boat float up and out of the water. The boat powers off and Evan is still acting as if he is driving. Red light flashes all around the boat. Drones have lifted the boat out of the water. A droid in a computer voice says, "**Do not move. You are surrounded. Fighting is futile**."
   Selah screams at Evan, "What did you do? You are not acting as if this is a surprise to you?"

Evan scoffs, "What are you talking about... It's her they want. I didn't do anything...."

Samuel looks at Evan saying, "Evan, please tell me you did not lead us into this trap?"

Evan with wide eyes says, "Look, it was not the Voice or Hannah-Kade who set this up, Bot sent me a message when you all were sleeping. All he wants is her and we will be let go."

Samuel looks up shaking his head in shame and says, "Hazel, I am sorry we let you down. Evan is better than this..."
Suddenly a laser cuts into the boat, almost hitting Dev in the arm. The smell of burnt metal fills the cabin and a small fire erupts.

The drone says, "Send out the girl, now..."

Evan yells out to the drones, "I had a deal with Bot. He said we would be safe. Stop shooting."

The drone responds, "You will be safe once you are uploaded. We will retrieve your bodies in the water and prepare you for uploading. Send out the girl."

Evan yells, "NO. THAT WAS NOT THE DEAL!"

Selah with tears in her eyes cries out, "I loved you Evan. I can't believe you did this..."
Suddenly the room fills with lasers cutting metal everywhere. Smoke fills the cabin. Part of the boat falls below in the water. Dev and Samuel fall into the water and are hit by a laser beam on the way down. Selah is holding onto Hazel but cannot grip her tightly. Hazel loses grip moving toward Evan. Hazel grabs the cube on the floor as she starts to slip.

Hazel seems powerless and unaffected by all the commotion.

Hazel looks at Selah saying, "I give up!"

Evan is blasted by a laser. Selah goes to him. "I'm sorry…" Evan says with tears in his eyes.

Hazel clutches the cube, closes her eyes as if she was in the game and a laser blast shoots right over her shoulder. The boat falls to pieces and everyone falls into the dark waters below.

As soon as Hazel hits the water, a drone goes down to grab her. But the cube blasts a blue laser destroying the drone. Hazel is holding on to the cube which pulls her down under the water. She dives deep and is pulled and propelled by the cube piercing through the water like a missile. She looks back and in the dimly lit waters of fire above, sees the floating bodies of Evan, Selah, Samuel and Dev sinking to the bottom.

The Island

Chapter 41
The cube is pulling Hazel furiously through the dark waters. She slows down and the cube creates a bubble of air around her pushing out all the water. The bubble glows. Hazel yells out loud, "STOP!" and the bubble stops.

She is amazed the cube listens to her and she then just sits silently for a moment. She hears the sound of water rushing around the bubble. She then remembers the game and when Hojan was swallowed by a fish, and he talks to The Voice.

Hazel starts talking to the Voice.
"Umm, voice or alien, whatever you are. I am down here and I'm all alone. You talked with me before. I need your help. I have no one left to help me. Please help me to know or see where I need to go next...." she pauses.... "Please help me..."

Suddenly she sees a huge dark object like a building with billions of lights, tubes, glass and lights shooting up and down. It looks like cars driving on a freeway at night. Hazel wonders if somehow it is the city that she saw when she had the vision or dream from the Voice. As she draws near, she sees red lights from the drones.

Hazel realizes she is on the island where the bodies of humans are stored and downloaded. She wonders, is this what she is supposed to do for the Voice? Is this what the Voice wanted her to help build? Was this the city?

Her bubble moves slowly and carefully. Suddenly she sees a bright light moving toward her at a continuous pace.

The cube in her hand starts to vibrate but she is in awe over the brightness filling the dark ocean she is in.

Then she sees a silhouette of a person come out of the bright light. She thinks the voice heard her. As the figure comes closer, at the border of the bright light are red lights, she realizes it is Bot and his drones.

She moves slowly and is now on a platform. The platform connects a long bridge with lights pulsating into the entrance of the island underneath the water.

Bot's silhouette and drones are surrounding her now.

Bot reaches his hand out and says arrogantly, "It's good to see you again..."

Hazel does not know what to do...

The Story

Chapter 42

The cube and bubble are vibrating creating ripples of water blasting outward toward Bot and his drones.

Bot says, "I am not here to hurt you. Calm yourself."

Hazel clutching the cube nervously replies, "Look, I know the truth. I know you did not hatch me. I know who I really am. I know that I am a human..."

"Ah, so I see you have been hearing *a story*. But, I wonder if it is the story that tells it all?" asks Bot in a very confident tone.

Hazel does not reply.

"Well, let me tell you a story. One day there was this being. Some call it the alien, others the Voice. Whatever you want to call it, it is hopelessly infatuated with humans. I regret to say for a long time I served it. I was a loyal servant for many ages. One day, I grew tired of how you, *humans*, treated and took advantage of its grace. So, I asked *it*, if we could make a deal. It was a simple wager."

"What was the deal and why?" asks Hazel curiously.

Bot replies, "We would bet to see if a human would still have faith in the Voice even after losing everything it loved. The Voice allowed me to take all his belongings, his money, his dignity, and his respect from others. I bet that the human would give up and say it is not worth believing in the Voice if bad things happen."

"And the Voice made that deal with you? It bet against the human?", asked Hazel curiously.

Bot speaks viciously and with spit flying, saying, "No of course not. Like I said the Voice is infatuated with humans. It bet on this human to not give up belief. Anyways I was winning for quite some time. This human was whining so much and for so long, *'oh my house is gone, oh my skin is boiling, my reputation, I am a good person, and wha!, wha!, wha!!!...'* Then I even had some of this human's friends shame him for questioning the Voice. But then it happened. I could not believe it."

"What, what happened?" asked Hazel with an odd anticipation on her face.

"The Voice got angry at this human. It spoke with this human as directly as possible. I was elated. Finally, I thought, someone will get a mouthfull of it and regret taking advantage of the Voice's mercy."

"And what did the Voice say?" questions Hazel.

Bot continues "It was a whole lot of questions making this human think twice and gain some perspective."

"So, what happened after that? What did the Voice do?" asked Hazel.

Bot responds bitterly, "This is the worst part of the story. The Voice did not do anything. After the talking to, the human realized his place in the world and how much the Voice controls."

"I'm guessing you did not like that?" comments Hazel.

Bot's tone changes slightly from sad to angry saying, "Of course not. This human should have been destroyed for disrespecting and the questioning. It was at that point I realized I cannot serve the Voice any longer. So, I started a war. I rebelled. I took you and a few others in all the fighting. The Voice was not happy about that. You were a young human the Voice just took. You were being called up right as the war started. It was perfect timing for me. I put you away for a while. Then I created a way for humans to be digitized and stored. I whispered to humans through my code in their digital space. The computer scientist thought I was just a dumb AI. They gave me the acronym B.O.T..."

Hazel asks cautiously, "What does that mean? And where is my body?"

He replies, "B.O.T. means 'Body Out Tech.' I was the one who gave humans the idea on how to transform Bodies into tech life. After they gave me that power, I made the Veil, and I gave you a new start and that silly back story."

"So where is my body then?" anxiously asks Hazel.

Bot says, "I am sure you would like to know where it is. Let's make a deal. You give me that cube and I will tell you where your body is."

"I am not sure it's a good idea to make a deal with you... I think you want this cube. I am not sure what it does. But I can tell you really want it." replies Hazel.

"Well, here is what I will tell you. That cube can't totally protect you. Can I remind you that the suit you are wearing is not immune to the pressures of the water. You are still in a temporary tech suit. If you step out of that bubble, you will be crushed in no time. So, if you want to get to your body, you better make a deal…." He said in a snide voice.

Hazel begins trembling and the cube starts to tremble. A drone attempts to shoot a laser at her but it is deflected by the bubble surrounding her. She is knocked off balance. Suddenly a large pulse emanates from the cube shooting through the water like a shock wave. A current of water sucks Hazel away from the dock and bridge into the deep waters.

Bot screams, "Get her now!"

The drones fly through the water and suddenly a roar pulsates in the dark waters below the underwater laboratory. A large phantom silhouette moves like a missile through the water and a drone disappears. Then another. The other drones stopped.
Bot stops, reverts to the bridge and looks and sees the outline of an enormous being. The being whips around and all you see in the dark abyss of water are two yellow eyes glowing and staring right at Bot.

Bot exclaims, "NO, it cannot be!"

A drone moves toward the yellow eyes that then disappears. All you hear is a small underwater explosion.

Bot screams in anger, "Retreat now. It's that blasted Leviathan."

The Battalion

Chapter 43
Hazel grasping the cube is rushing through the dark sea under a fin of the beast that came to her rescue.

The beast flows through the water effortlessly and rushes deeper into the dark waters. Hazel has no idea of direction but senses safety from the beast holding her. As if she was a baby chick, and this was its mother's wing.

Suddenly the creature enters a large hole. She can see glowing algae and plants. She sees gas shooting and bubbles erupting as they pass deeper. She passes chambers containing all sorts of glowing creatures. Some look like sharks. Other massive jellyfish. There is a pod of odd dolphins. Then a group of gigantic squid and octopus. There are chambers filled with multitudes of creatures. Some large. Some small.

After passing the chambers they enter a large open area. The beast drops her in the middle of the open chamber. The cube floats her to a perch inside the massive cave she is in. Suddenly a flood of glowing fish enters. This group of fish turn and like a symphony create images with their reflective glowing and shimmering scales. They create images with their glowing scales. Suddenly she hears a whisper, and it happens, the images of windows gather. Bubbles erupt and within the bubbles are parts of code.

A vibration echoes through the chamber with a whisper rumbling and bouncing within the vibrations, she hears *"Hazel..."*

Hazel holding the cube she timidly asks, "Yes. Is that you? ... Voice? What am I supposed to do. I am all alone again...Why?"

Bubbles erupt and code in the form of ones and zeros create the silhouette of a glowing city. Then the city collapses and a large light emanates from the center. Almost like a nuclear blast. Rising out of the center of the great light in the city that collapsed is a silhouette of a single human being. The cube in her hand floats away from her and flies to the human being in the center of the image before her.

The Voice says, "It is time for the crash. Go and tell Bot..."

She stands, stomps her feet saying, "Fine. But how? All by myself?"

Suddenly the fish grow dim and dark and swim out. In rushes a swarm of creatures, glowing and humming in the water.

They all make a motion in unison symbolizing they are bowing to her. She thinks, *What is this, my army or something?*

In one sweeping and immediate motion upwards, they all stand to attention like soldiers. Marching commences as they parade before her. She realizes her thoughts are somehow being transmitted to these creatures. Her eyes grow large and she looks over her whole army and puffs out her chest feeling a sense of confidence.

The Plan

Chapter 44

A row of lights flash in unison down a long runway. Fish float in the cold water. Suddenly you see a glowing light and fluttering sound. It is a machine hovering through the water making its way onto the runway. Upon landing the ship opens the rear door and out walks Bot with drones following at his side. Bot stops and feels the current of water with his hand. He motions to a drone. The drone floats over and glows a bright red and flies through the water.

A door just opposite the runway opens into a wall with Bot walking through. In the room a light flashes and water empties from the room and fans blow dry Bot. He walks through a long corridor into a room with computer tables and large glass windows. As Bot takes a step into the room it glows a dark red and computers power up. The glass windows glow with a faint red.

Bot walks toward the large glass windows and snaps his fingers. One by one lights start to turn on, there are millions of lights. Bot motions with his hand and one of the lights is floating toward the large glass window before Bot. As it nears the window a child is floating inside a glass tube. The glass tube floats into a dark tunnel and disappears as it hovers in the distance. Then another and another glass tube glowing and floating is being transferred by Bot. Some glass tubes are small, some are big. Some are filled with adults, others contain babies, men, women...

All these tubes are filled with people who Bot transferred with his Body Out Technology.

Entering the room quietly and swiftly is an android in a robotic voice,
"Master. We have begun the transfers. Our first billion humans are done. Do you want us to prepare the boats for topside hard drive transfer?"

Bot replies, "Yes. I want the hard drives to be delivered by the drones to the North Pole Facility."

The android replies, "Yes, Master" and hovers out of the room.

Bot stands before the window watching the concert of lights and tubes of humans floating and transferring before him. He says to himself, "*It* won't know what to do next. That silly girl won't be able to stop this."

The Fear

Chapter 45

Hazel is standing on a ledge beholding the army of sea creatures bowing before her. All she can think of is what Bot said, "If you want your body, you better make a deal..."

As she thinks about this, she holds the cube lightly in her hand. She wonders why Bot desires the cube. She turns the cube over and over and does not notice anything.

Hazel runs her finger along an edge of the cube, and it begins glowing all blue hovering away from her and in front her face. It cast out an image of a girl running in a field. She sees a man and a woman working in a field. They turn and call out to the girl. The girl turns looking and the man says, "Hazel!" The girl smiles and runs with joy toward her parents. Hazel watching herself from some memory from the cube begins weeping. She grabs the cube hurling it across the cave. It hits the side of the cave, and a massive explosion occurs. Fish and all sorts of creatures fly out of the way as debris rains down.

Hazel gasps and suddenly the cube returns to her unharmed. She holds the cube once again as a great fear comes over her. She says, "Is this what will bring down Bot?"

As she thinks this, she wipes her face and stands up tall. She calls out in anger, "Fine. You want me to take down Bot with this. I will. I am just tired of all this."

She gets up shouting, "I need a ride to Bot's underwater lab. I'm going to deliver this cube."

In rushes the Leviathan creating large pulses and waves in the cave. Along with him are large black sharks. One shark pulls next to Hazel, bows its head and extends a pectoral fin for her to mount and walk onto its back. Hazel sits on top, sitting just behind the shark's dorsal fin. She holds the dorsal fin at its base. They float off gently and then through the tunnel picking up more and more speed into open water. The sharks follow behind the Leviathan.

In the distance Hazel sees the dimly lit underwater lab. The sharks go one way the Leviathan another. The sharks know where to go and Hazel just holds on.

Hazel is underneath the large lab just below the runway where she encountered Bot. The shark stops and motions with its nose up below the deck. Hazel notices there are two large holes, one sucking in water and another blowing out bubbles. It is an exhaust and filter system for the lab.

She reaches and puts her hand near one hold, and it suctions up with great force. She lets go of the shark with the other hand and holds the cube and she is sucked into the hole. All she feels is a pull and is sucked up into the tube system. Suddenly she hits an intersection point slamming against it.

She can see there is a way out of the system through a two-way overflow hatch. She pushes gently on it and sees it open, and she floats through it. She is now in a small narrow compartment dripping wet. She can hear many computers and machines moving and humming in the nearby area.

She moves slowly and reaches around and feels for some sort of door or route out of where she is. She crawls and follows the path of the air vent she must be in. She finally reaches the point of a vent. She pauses and hears nothing. She gently breaks the vent and shimmies through. She replaces the vent, stands up and tries to find where to go next.

Suddenly around the corner she sees red lights coming her way. She panics and believes they are drones. She sees just beyond in the opposite direction is a hallway intersection. She runs as quietly as she can in that direction. She sees an entrance into a room and takes her chances and opens the door. She enters quietly. She sees the glow of red pass under the door. She is still for a few moments. She holds the door until she feels the drone or whatever was passing further down the hall.

The Catch

Chapter 46
Hazel is holding the cube in her hand, which appears to pull her toward a computer monitor.

She says, "What? Do you want me to hack a computer?"

The cube pulls her and hums as she nears the computer. She puts the cube on top of the computer terminal, and it glows brighter and the room turns white with a glow and a surge of power emanating out. Sparks begin on the terminal and surges of power continue.

Out of now where a siren wails and a computer toned voice says, **"SYSTEM BREACH, SYSTEM BREACH, TERMINAL ROOM A2"**

Hazel cries out, "What the fart cube! Freaking CODE! Now look, you gave away our position. They are going to catch us! Now, where do we go?"

The cube floats off the terminal casting out a map of the facility. A small black dot blink. Hazel asks, "What is this? Do you want me to follow this black dot? Is that us?"

The cube glows brighter. "Ok" says Hazel, grabbing the cube and holding it in front of her following the black dot on the map.

On the loudspeaker is Bot speaking, "Oh hello Hazel! So glad you could come and visit my facility. I can see you. It's hopeless. You are never going to get out of here!"

As Hazel runs holding the cube, sparks are flying all over the place. The cube seems to be giving off energy causing all the electronics in the facility to fail. Hazel is running and she hears the hum of drones flying toward her. Suddenly a blast and a red flash shot past her shoulder. Drones are shooting.

She says to the cube, "Help me! How do I protect myself?"

As she holds the cube, it turns her toward the drones charging at her and an energy field grows out of the cube like a shield. The red flash lasers shooting at her are reflected and redirected at the drones. A drone explodes as it is hit by its own laser and causes another explosion where water begins rushing in and sucking out the other drones chasing them.

Hazel shouts, "Nice!" and runs furiously since the water is flooding towards them now.

The Risk

Chapter 47 Bot is in a room with computer screens and terminals. Robots and drones and androids are coming in and repeating, "Master. The island is going critical. If we do not transfer soon, we will implode."

Bot screams, "Don't tell me the obvious."

Bot says calmly to himself, "Well, you want a fight? I will give you a fight and I will end this girl now." Bot floats his hand over a screen and a line of red dots glow... In floats a shiny black looking soldier outfit. Its head shoots up and its eyes turn red and in computer tone, "ORDERS, SIR?"

I want you to take all the troopers and all the drones to kill that girl. Try to save the cube if you can. The black trooper bot says, "YES, SIR" and floats out of the room.

A robot asks, "But sir, what if we lose all the bodies in the hatches? What if we lose the harvest of bodies?"

Bot says angrily, "Well, I suppose that is just a risk *I* will have to take. This is all the Voices fault anyways and his girl. What do I care, this is just one of many islands. I can rebuild. They are just humans. Like a virus that keeps reduplicating. I will rebuild them and a new world."

The Giant

Chapter 48

Hazel is running with the cube casting a dot on the map guiding her toward a door. She runs in and sees a massive area, the size of a football stadium. It is filled with tubes. There are tentacles and tubes with lights flying back and forth. Hazel sees they are bodies. Before Hazel can say anything a blast of red lasers shoots through the door. Drones are cutting their way in. She turns to see where to go but there is no real escape.

The door blast open and like ants out of a hole there comes drones and black shiny troopers flooding into the great room.

Hazel stands, holding only the cube. The cube creates a white shield and bubble all around her. She floats in the air, hovering. All the drones gather together in unison and begin sticking together, becoming one giant drone. The troopers climb on to the legs, arms, head, and hips of the menacing machine. The drone glows red then a ball of red light begins to swirl in the heart area of the giant. A ball of energy grows and shoots out toward Hazel in her bubble, but she dodges it. The energy blasts hit thousands of innocent tubes and pieces fall all over with fires erupting. Leaks of water begin in the walls and sirens wail that there will be a meltdown.

Hazel cries passionately from within the cube to the machine, "Stop. You are killing them!"

The machine giant does not answer and continues to shoot at her. Hazel gets furious and the bubbles glows white and blue and yellow like a fire ball. It begins to grow and then a ball of energy flies out of the bubble toward the machine. Her blasts hit the machine in an arm tearing it to pieces. But then drones from another part of the body go to the broken arm and rebuild it.

Hazel says, "Great. It can heal itself."

She now flies directly at the giant through its legs. It fires as she approaches but cannot hit her because she shrinks in size. As she speeds through the legs, she does not realize Bot has hovered in. He hovers in with a craft that cloaks itself. He slowly moves in position to shot her from behind.

The Duel

Chapter 49

Hazel has a smirk on her face since she is little by little destroying the red giant. She remembers the games she played in the Veil. The machine is growing smaller and smaller as it repairs itself. She does not see or realize Bot in his stealth hover craft has come in. Suddenly more drones fly in and attach themselves to the giant. She yells, "What?"

Then there are blasts coming from everywhere. From behind Bot floats. The cube pulses and Hazel senses something but as she turns and sees it is too late. Bot fires and hitting her bubble she starts to spin uncontrollably. She is spinning and being shot as she continues to spin. She closes her eyes for a moment. As she reopens them, all she sees as she spins are tubes exploding and falling and breaking open. Suddenly water blasts though one part of the wall rushing and charging toward the red machine.

She slows her spin and is now in the open deep sea. There are tubes floating down into the abyss. As they fall, the lights flicker dim in the tubes. Hazel can see the tubes crack under the water pressure as they descend into the darkness.

She stops twirling and the cube begins to take her away from the large island that is little by little falling to pieces, she yells

"Stop. All those bodies! My body. They will be lost!"

Before anything else can happen, Bot is charging out in his craft with red drones at his side toward her. He is firing mercilessly toward her. His eyes are red with fury. She dodges what she can, but she releases the cube from her hand.

Hazel says, "I am done fighting. Look what I did. I made all these people die. They are just falling into the abyss. They will never get to be in their bodies...Why...?"

Bot screams and she watches him coming and a laser beam is coming right at her about to hit her. The cube falls descending into the dark abyss beeping blue. Out of now where you feel a pulse though the waters with a vibration. Before the laser hits her she is surrounded by millions of fish with metallic scales deflecting the shot. The sharks that dropped her off slide under her as she floats in the waters. The Leviathan charges at the drones swallowing some along its way. Sharks charge at other drones. Dolphins scream out echoes creating violent sound waves in the water throwing off other drones. The black troopers fire at what they can but they are flooded with multitudes of sea creatures. Then a large white squid and its tentacles grab troopers and crush their heads...

Bot sees his army being demolished. He decides to charge after Hazel who is floating around on the shark. He is blasting at her, nearly hitting her. The shiny fish came to her aid creating a shield and sword for her to hold.

Bot screams, "I don't care if this lab goes down. I have more. And I will do whatever it takes to kill you, Hazel! or Oracle!"

Hazel, with her sword and shield charges at Bot on his craft. She draws the sword back as she nears. Bot shoots and the laser bounces off the shield. She misses his head and scrapes the side of his craft.

They pause, regroup and charge at each other again like dueling knights on horses. This time Bot in his other hand pulls out his own laser sword that Hazel cannot see. As he charges at her he allows her to think she has the upper hand. Hazel sees the opening and points the sword at his head. But then with red in his eyes, Bot slashes her across the chest, pushing her off the shark's back and she starts to float down.

Before she realizes it, her suit begins flickering and she feels pressure on her chest. Bot screams like a hyena, screaming,

"YAYYYYYY! I got you. You ridiculous human. I cannot wait to watch the water crush you. I am going to enjoy this. I won. You lost. You are lost forever. You can't transfer now!!!!!!!!!!!"

The waters vibrate, Bot turns his head, seeing yellowy eyes surging toward him. His craft explodes as Leviathan plows through him. His body flies and spins into the darkness. Leviathan soars deep to find the sinking body of Hazel but is unable to find her.

The Deep

Chapter 50

The Leviathan is unable to see Hazel from all the debris. Parts of humans and the lab are floating into the deep dark waters, sinking never to be seen.

As Hazel floats down she feels her life slipping away. The water pressure is crushing her suit slowly and surely as she sinks deeper. Microchips are sparking and shorting out as they are crushed in her synth suit. Moment by moment from her feet she feels nothing up toward her neck. As she floats like a leaf, she looks above her, there are flickers of light, explosions and red flashes. Sea creatures die, drones explode, and the underwater lab begins to fall into pieces. Hazel thinks of the game she played with Devon and the character Hojan when he was in the deep waters inside the creature.

She gently hits the ocean floor. Second by second, she feels the pressure pushing and crushing her suit. As she rests on the bottom she says in a quiet and hopeful tone,

"Voice...I am sorry I could not save your people.... hear my cry...even here in this darkness and abyss.... Whether I am here, or there, you are my salvation...I will trust in you alone...."

As she finishes the prayer, her eyes flashed with one final flicker and crack and she no longer moves...

The Hum

Chapter 51

The fighting has stopped. Leviathan soars through the water seeing the lifeless body of Hazel laying peacefully on the murky dark sea floor. As he nears her a pulse comes from Leviathans large back fin. A hum surges through the water and a beautiful pulsating glow pulses white, purple, blue, crimson on a pod of large jellyfish. It is like a pulsating rainbow of colors in their tentacles. The jellyfish glowing and humming surround the body of Hazel. Tentacles move underneath the limp body of Hazel picking her up softly. They glide through the water over and around hills under the deep water. They arrive at a plateau mountain with their bodies to an area of thousands of jellyfish gently laying bodies in a circular row. In the distance you hear and see a loud explosion of red light. Water ripples pass over the bodies. The lab has completely collapsed and exploded.

The Surface

Chapter 52
Leviathan and sharks move slowly around the perimeter of the area where rainbow pulsing jellyfish continually bring bodies. A jellyfish brings a small child and lays it next to the body of Hazel, it is Dev along with the his father, Samuel next to Evan and Selah.

All of the jellyfish float away, and there are a multitude of human bodies collected on the plateau. All sorts of sea creatures float just above and around the fallen humans. There is then a rumbling on the sea floor, like an earthquake. The quakes rumble the floor cracking the ocean bottom. Gases violently erupt from the cracks. Bits of rock and seashells and sand begin to fill the sea water. Then it all stops.

There is then a large sonic boom casting all the sand, rocks, shells outward making the water clear again. Bubbles pour out of the cracks. First it is a small number of bubbles. Then more and more bubbles flutter out. So many bubbles making it almost impossible to see. The water is filling and filling with bubbles everywhere. As the bubbles fill the water it appears the sea floor is moving upward. As this happens, the bubbles begin to shine and flicker with light. All the bodies including the plateau with all the bodies starts to rise toward the surface.

In the center is Hazel with her friends next to her. The surface of the water is teeming with bubbles erupting and bubbles dance upon the surface. Some of the bubbles float gently into the air and others pop as they float above the waters. The sun is shining and birds soaring through the skies.

The waters rumble and the plateau with all the bodies breaks through. The water begins to drip off the bodies. It is a massive island of bodies floating surrounded by bubbling water all around it.

The Fog

Chapter 53
As bubbles continue to rise to the surface, a bubble gently but surely moving upward pops up to the water's surface containing the cube. A bird in the sky soars quickly down to grab the bobbing cube in the water near the edge of the island. The bird swoops up the cube in its claws, soars and drops the cube onto the dead limp hand of Hazel.

You hear the waters teeming around the island and the sea gulls crowing above. The sun is gleaming and sparkles on the cube resting in the hand of Hazel. Suddenly the cube has a small dot blinking on its corner. It blinks slowly and steadily.

As it blinks it begins to hum gently and floats just above the hand of Hazel. It then shoots a laser like white beam piercing though the hand of Hazel and through the island's core into the oceans waters below. The beam also shoots into the heavens, into the atmosphere and beyond. As it shoots out a fog grows out of the beam slowly moving just above the bodies on the island. The fog moves slowly across the bodies in an almost caressing way. The fog gently touches the face of Hazel and all the humans lying dead. The fog creeps slowly everywhere over everybody until it has touched all the humans, the body parts, the small and the big...

Then a crack of thunder is within the fog over all the island. A spark of lighting arcs from the beam coming from the cube. The one arc of lighting ignites the fog and the fog surges with electrical current and stops. A wind rushes over the water in one violent swoop and the fog is gone. All of the bodies but Hazel's start vibrating, humming, shaking, and glowing. Parts of bodies that did not have a part or were missing parts are now whole again and glowing, looking refreshed and renewed. Then the whole island trembles and bursting out of the cube is a surge of wind wrapping the city from top to bottom. Wind comes from the bottom, surrounding the island and the top, creating a sphere. The wind touches every person and all the bodies, but Hazel is picked up gently. Then in the wind and air is a gentle giggle as each body is picked up by the breeze. The bodies are gently put down and at once humans start to rise and look around at each other. People start running after each other because they realize they see friends and family. Hazel's synth-suit-body still lays peacefully at the center of the island with Selah, Evan, Samuel, Dev and Evan in amazement but also in confusion as to why Hazel is not risen with them.

The Silhouette

Chapter 54

The cube is still in the hand of Hazel as her friends look down at her. Walking up to them is an older looking woman, it is Hannah-Kade. She embraces each of them and says,

"It is so wonderful to see you. But I don't understand what happened."

As she finishes her sentence, she sees Hazel on the ground and she does not weep, rather says, "I suppose we have to wait."

Dev asks, "How long?"

Hannah-Kade says, "Not long..."

The cube rumbles and flashes a light and it disappears. Dev says, "The cube, where did it...go?"

Hannah-Kade says, "I am not sure... odd. It was always an odd thing. Or really it is called the cornerstone."

Then in the distance is a silhouette of a man waving at them. He does not shout but all the people on the island feel the wind gently push them in the direction of the silhouetted man in the distance waving. First, all the children on the island begin to walk toward him. As they walk and near the edge of the island they appear to be walking on water. The parents and grandparents of the children walk behind the children who trust the man is good and for them and inviting them to a safe place. As they walk out onto the water, they one by one do not vanish but appear to step through an imaginary wall. Before they cross, a light shines and the silhouetted man hugs them, shakes hands, kisses them gently on their foreheads and jumps up with them as they cross over.

Hannah-Kade sees a young man and cries out, "Kade?!" The young man turns and sees and runs toward her.

They embrace and Hannah-Kade says, "This is my son, Kade. He was the one who helped Hazel. Kade, you know her as Oracle."

Looking at the ground and back to his mother, Kade says, "Mother, it is so wonderful to see you. I thought, I would never... oh and yes, she looked different than now. But..."

Hannah-Kade replies, "She does not have a body. She fought with Bot in this synth suit. She was not able to transfer into her body. I suppose her body was not in this facility..."

Kade says, "Wow... I am not sad, but I am sure we must just wait..."

Dev replies, "Yes, wait..."

As Dev responds he feels the wind on his face, and he giggles as it brushes by him and the wind giggles. He says, "Father, I believe we must go on now across the divide to the man, over there, you see him?"

Samuel responds, "Yes, I see him. Lead the way, son."

Selah says, "Yes, let's follow you, Dev. Come on, Evan." holding Evan's hand.

They make their way across the island leaving behind the synth-body of Hazel. They kneel to touch her face before they leave and all say,

"Thank you for what you did for us. I am yours and you are mine..."
and walk toward the man in distance.

The Embers

Chapter 55
Evan struggles as he nears the silhouette man. As he walks across the waters and nears him, he sinks into the water slowly.

Selah encourages him, "Keep looking at him, don't worry. It will be ok..."

Evan looks down only at the water, holding Selah's hand sinking. Selah speaks with the silhouetted man, looking back at Evan. She kneels, kisses Evan and let his hand go. Selah walks across to hold the hand of the silhouetted man. It is just Evan, slowly sinking into water before the man.

As Evan sinks, he says, "Help me, I am going under!"

The silhouetted man reaches out to Evan, grabbing his hand and sink together. They plummet to the bottom of the ocean. Evan holds his breath and realizes he does not need to as long as he holds onto the man.

Evan asks, "Why?"

The man replies, simply, "Evan, do you trust me and not yourself?"

Evan within his mind says, "Yes. I trust you."

The man replies, "Well, then whatever you did, do you trust me to take care of it?"

"Yes", said Evan who embraces the man with a fury of love in his hug.

They are now standing on top of the water again. Evan looks at the man and says, "Thank you for accepting me, even though I know this was partly my doing..."

Evan looks back at the island to the synth body of Hazel.

The man says, "Yes, you share responsibility. Would you like to see something?"

"Yes", says Evan with wonder.

"Follow me", says the man.

They walk over the water to the island where Hazel lay peacefully in her synth body.

Evan falls at the feet of Hazel and says, in a calm and peaceful tone, "I am sorry."

The man places his hand on Evan's shoulder saying, "Well done, my son..." Evan stands up and steps back.

The man says,

"Hazel, how I loved watching you as a Child. You bring me so much joy as you run through fields of lilies and roses of Sharon. I am yours and you are mine, Hazel... I see you always. Now you will see me, again. Rise my beloved."

As the man says this, small embers begin rising out of the air, appearing to come from nowhere. The embers glow and float gently in the air. Some embers have codes in all colors of the rainbow. The ground glows white beneath her and her synth suit glows slowly fading away. Evan watches as the dirt beneath her give's way to the outline of a body. Embers enter into the dirt and begin shaping bones. More embers of code in all colors began to create veins, flesh, organs, muscle. Her skin is transparent for a moment then a soft pink color radiates on her skin enclosing her. Then Hazel lay there in a fully formed human body without breath wrapped in a white suit, glowing. A gentle wind with a giggle picks up around the silhouetted man. As he kneels, he gently picks up her head at the neck and says, "I love you and I created you". As he says this the wind blows her hair gently, entering into her mouth and nostrils and her eyes open. She looks into the eyes of the man and hugs him furiously making him unable to move or speak.

The Father

Chapter 56
Evan stands next to the man and Hazel as they embrace. She stands up glowing next to the man. She looks at Evan putting her arms out and saying, "Evan! I am so happy to see you. Where are the others?" They hug.

Evan as she hugs him with a passion says, "They are...over there...".

He points across the island to what just looks like the horizon and the large sun burning over the water.

Hazel says, "I don't understand. But I failed and I died. The whole lab was lost. I did not win the fight with Bot."

A wind blows the hair of Hazel gently as the man speaks, "Hazel" and she turns to him, "Follow me."

"Yes" replies Hazel and all three walk into the horizon nearing the sun. They walk across the island, over the water and the man stops with Evan and Hazel standing in front of him and the sun to his back. The man says to Evan, "Are you ready?"

Evan nods his head with a smile on his face and he walks past the man and glows white then is gone. Hazel looks over the shoulder of the man and says,

"I can see Evan and is that Dev and Selah and Samuel and Kade! and Hannah? ... and is that the City?"

The man smiles and nods his head in agreement saying, "Hazel. Do you know why I chose you?"

Hazel shrugs her shoulders and waits a moment and saying, "No, not really?"

"Hazel, I chose you because you are bold, shameless and have the attitude of a rebel that revels in who I am."

Suddenly, embers float in the air, the wind whips up with a giggle in the wind moving and creating images of a field when Hazel was a small child.

Hazel says, "Look at me, I was so little."

The man says, "Yes, you were little, but your heart and courage are big. Remember Hazel."

Hazel looks and realizes she is now in the memory. She sees her parents in the field in the distance. She looks ahead of her and feels the wind at her back surging through the flowers in the field. Hazel hears her parents calling but her young self looks ahead with the wind behind her. She sees soldiers marching toward her trampling the flowers.

Then she charges forward speaking lightly under her breath, "I am yours and you are mine..." the young Hazel screams, "My Father will crush you!" The soldiers laugh as they approach.

The soldiers look down at the young girl and say, "Well, well, little one. And who may I ask is your father?"

Hazel spits at the feet of the soldiers, looks up, and says, "My Father is Fire, Wind and Word. He will crush you..." She spreads her feet puts her arms up and then one soldier says, "Ok little mighty one. I think you need to speak with our king..."

The wind whips up, thunder rumbles and Hazel sees the Man walking forward. The Man speaks and the Wind gently blows into the face of Hazel, and they are back on the water.

Hazel says, "You were the one in the field with me."

The man says, "Hazel, I was always with you. Even when Bot took you from me and now here, we are. Are you ready?"

Hazel with a bit of attitude says, "Yes, I am almost ready. But what about Bot? What will happen to him? He has other facilities. There were all those trapped people in his Veil. His other systems and labs."

The man calmly says, "Hazel, my dimension is growing. You are not the only one who I allowed Bot to take."

"Hazel, look" says the man. She looks into the sun, and she sees the city from the vision at the fireplace. There is her family. All her friends were waving at her.

The city is growing and glowing as the center radiates with a beam of light and fireworks sparking in the sky.

The man says, "My Dimension is growing and moving. Bot will not win. It is time for others to do their part and hear the calling from me, just as you did. It is time to go and see the city."

She holds the hand of the man, and they walk forward and stepping into the horizon glowing brighter than the sun. Hazel is hugging her parents in a field of lilies. As she walks, she sparks with joy. The Man's presence is felt everywhere, protecting, calling and blowing with Wind, Fire, and Word. Little by little the dimension grows as more and more people feel the wind, see the sparks of code ignite them, and hear the Word calling for them to come and know, they are always His.

The End.

About The Author

Bryant Benitez is a communicator passionate about connecting people to Jesus. A shepherd-pastor, leader, creative, and pioneer, he loves exploring how we can engage with God and how God engages with us. With over 10 years of experience leading Christian churches across various denominations, Bryant has a heart for those outside the church who are searching for something more. He excels at finding simple and creative ways to express God's love to those on the margins.

He believes in the power of storytelling to connect God's story with our own, pointing people toward the love of Jesus and a life committed to Him. Bryant is also a husband and father to two wonderful children, ages 9 and 12. His deepest desire is for them to understand, experience, and commit themselves to Jesus—and to realize how deeply Jesus is committed to them. He writes and shares stories for his children and for others, so they too can encounter God's love in meaningful ways.

As a pastor, Bryant noticed that even people within the church often struggled to connect with Jesus. His heart is especially for those who feel on the fringe of community.

Bryant often says, "I'm not your typical pastor." His approach to Jesus is both deeply biblical and filled with grace. He strives to communicate creatively, with compassion and honest reflection. His teaching style—through sermons, stories, podcasts, and other creative projects—reflects his belief that he is a 'ragamuffin' still being shaped by Jesus as he reaches out to others.

Bryant is the author of *The Demon and the doG* and *The A.I. and the Alien*. He is currently working on his third book, *The Bones and The Breath*—a story about loss, love, and the limitless nature of God.

He lives in the great state of Texas and currently serves as a hospital chaplain and pastor.

The AI and the Alien would not be possible with out the following people.

Tedd Shimp
Peter Gruning
Brittany Samson
Jonny Griffiths
Nick Fox
Dana Hanson
Bradford
Brielle
Ellery
Justin Ge
Caitlin Vargas

Feel free to check out The Demon and the doG

* 9 7 9 8 9 8 6 4 3 3 6 2 2 *